AGAINST THE WALL

STORIES

AGAINST THE WALL

STORIES

ALBERTO ROBLEST

English translation by Nicolás Kanellos

Arte Público Press
Houston, Texas

Against the Wall is made possible through a grant from the National Endowment for the Arts. We are thankful for its support.

Recovering the past, creating the future

Arte Público Press
University of Houston
4902 Gulf Fwy, Bldg 19, Rm 100
Houston, Texas 77204-2004

Cover design by Mora Design
Cover photograph by Enrique Chiu

Names: Roblest, Alberto, 1962- author. | Kanellos, Nicolas, translator.
Title: Against the wall : stories / Alberto Roblest ; English translation by Nicolas Kanellos.
Description: Houston, Texas : Arte Público Press, [2021] | This selection of short stories has not been published in Spanish. | English translation of Spanish text. | Summary: "In the prologue to this inventive collection, the exhausted protagonist finally reaches the doors to paradise after an arduous journey, but the longed-for entrance doesn't have a handle or keyhole and there's no bell or intercom. He considers climbing over it, but the wall reaches to the sky. He thinks of magic words that might open it and even kicks it, to no avail. The long, difficult trip has brought him to nothing except a concrete wall surrounded by desert. The characters in these seventeen stories find themselves with their backs against the wall, whether literally or figuratively. They run the gamut from undocumented immigrants to faded rock and soap-opera stars and even the Washington Monument. The eyes of the world focus on the blackened obelisk, which is covered in millions of insects, as government forces attempt to deal with this national emergency! Several pieces deal with people who are lost or long to go back in time. In one, Ramirez wakes up disoriented to discover he-along with untold others-is trapped in a bus terminal, unable to leave the Lost & Found area that's piled high with thousands of suitcases, trunks, backpacks and packages. Strange dreams pervade the nights of others. A female monster, la chingada, chases a man through a maze full of garbage and starving children, and he wonders if he should just confront his destiny. A worker falls asleep on the subway after a triple shift and dreams he's in a pool with Death swimming towards him. Exploring topics such as immigration, corruption and police abuse, Roblest expertly depicts the loneliness and uncertainty of people struggling to survive, but who yearn for something more elusive. These moving portraits reflect the lives of those who must breach the walls-physical, social, political or cultural-blocking their paths"—Provided by publisher.
Identifiers: LCCN 2021027348 (print) | LCCN 2021027349 (ebook) | ISBN 9781558859258 (trade paperback) | ISBN 9781518506659 (epub) | ISBN 9781518506666 (kindle edition) | ISBN 9781518506673 (pdf)
Subjects: LCSH: Roblest, Alberto, 1962—Translations into English. | LCGFT: Short stories.
Classification: LCC PQ7298.28.O2397 A7413 2021 (print) | LCC PQ7298.28.O2397 (ebook) | DDC 863/.64—dc23
LC record available at https://lccn.loc.gov/2021027348
LC ebook record available at https://lccn.loc.gov/2021027349

21 22 23   4 3 2 1

Table of Contents

Prologue

for Tomás Rivera . . . And the Earth Did Not Devour Him

They said that was the way. I spent many days crossing mountains and valleys, crossing two rivers and a desert mountain range, where there was nothing but dilapidated adobe houses, some tattered windmills and junked cars covered in sand. I finally arrived, shed my backpack and stretched my arms, took off my boots to let my feet rest. It had been a long trip. I wiped my brow with a tissue and walked up to the door, touched it to make sure it was real. I smiled. I had arrived . . . finally.

I found myself right in front of the door to paradise, a glorious entryway, a beautiful door. I knocked with my knuckles, then my fist, then with both of them. I searched for the door handle, the keyhole in the lock, but couldn't find it, nor a bell or an intercom. Perhaps the door was locked from the inside. I pushed it hoping it would give, but no. Then I thought it might be a sliding door and tried again, but the door seemed unmovable. I thought about climbing over it, but the walls seemed to reach up into the sky and the door presented no footholds. I tried pushing again, this time with all I had. It occurred to me that in many tales doors open with magic code words or rhymes. I traced out what would be a code in the dust at the foot of the door. I came up with tongue twisters, songs, my grandmother's favorite sayings, I screamed. . . . At one point, I desperately kicked the damn door that was looking more like the entry to a bunker or a fortress. Everything I tried was useless. Sweating, I decided to sit down on the ground. I guessed that the only recourse was to wait for someone to exit and I'd scramble inside, although that was really a dumb idea: Who the hell would want to leave paradise? I put my boots back on, I stood up and walked a couple of kilometers looking for the terminus of the wall. I came back and tried to come up with some other ideas. I was annoyed. There was nothing I could do but wait and grieve. I sat down on a boulder with the hopes of someone with a key or password coming along and I could go in with him. I took a sip out of my canteen—there wasn't much water left, nor food. I looked one way, then the other way, nothing except for the door and the great wall. The door was at the end of the road I had traveled. From one side to the other ran the concrete wall, the desert, nobody, nothing.

BLACKENED OBELISK

1

The morning sun revealed yellow plastic police tape around the whole mall area, from Pennsylvania Avenue to Independence, and from there up to 6th. There were about a hundred cops and criminologists, fire trucks, ambulances. They were deployed because the obelisk, the Washington Monument, was covered in insects, which were first thought to be ants or locusts, but as the morning light shined it became obvious: they were roaches, roaches of all sizes. The first person to report the strange event was Emerson Martínez, a bicycle cop on his last round. At first, he thought blown spotlights had darkened the monument that was the pride of the city and symbol of the entire country. But as he approached, he had other ideas: someone had covered the spotlight with some type of film or, worse, an evildoer had splashed black paint on the monument's surfaces, and if that was the case, that could not be anything else but an act of terrorism. He kept thinking. Perhaps it was some type of art installation created by crazy artists who had been rejected by the arts council. . . . What a surprise it was when he got within ten yards and discovered that the dark stain was moving, as if swaying to the rhythm of the hypnotic sound it emitted. Martínez did not know what to think. The stain was insects— cockroaches to be precise. He dropped his bike to the ground, approached cautiously, took out his gun and chambered a bullet, then stopped to carefully examine the thing. No doubt about it: roaches. He'd seen enough of them in his kitchen, in the kitchen of cheapo restaurants, at the police station, at homes and rent-controlled apartments and even at old Georgetown mansions.

He spoke into his radio once again, making it official to his supervisor at the station. Officer George Luca listened. Not believing his ears at first, he made Martínez repeat the information several times. Thousands of roaches were covering the obelisk from peak to base.

"Shit, that is bad news," Luca said.

It certainly was, and it was coming at the end of his shift on the Friday before the Memorial three-day weekend. Gritting his teeth, George Luca called his captain, who decided to talk to Martínez directly. He listened to the patrolman attentively and then passed the bad news on to his superiors, who then showed the same skepticism and had Martínez repeat the story a few more times. Not twenty minutes had gone by when the police chief, in person, burst into the Capitol Hill station and asked Luca if the bicycle cop who had reported the incident was sound of mind. He then asked if the cop used drugs or was under the influence of prescription medicine, along with Martínez's badge number.

"No, boss. Martínez has nothing like that on his record . . . an' he got high grades at the academy . . . and, uh . . . he's been in great health."

Strange, the police chief thought as he pulled out his cellphone and asked his close confidants, who were finishing rounds downtown, to head for the scene of the crime. In less than fifteen minutes they had confirmed the initial report:

thousands, no millions, of dark roaches were all over the monument, from top to bottom. The bad news was soon made public and began to circulate from one side of town to the other, through official channels, on TV, the internet, virally.

2

Once the news hit the internet, there was a surge in memes, fake news and off-color jokes, as well as conspiracy theories. Never before had so many sirens been heard in Washington DC, not even at the attempted assassination of President Ronald Reagan or the inauguration of Barack Obama. By the time the sun had fully risen, everything was different: city streets were deserted, as were the main highways; schools and colleges shuttered, along with government offices; tourist offices paralyzed; social and cultural events throughout the city canceled; the Pentagon and other security agencies crazed; the daily newspapers rushing to change the lead stories; the Metro and other public transportation delayed; physical as well as viral traffic erratic; the local radio stations flooded with calls and numerous news blogs; the politicians jockeying to present their best face to the public; and the rubberneckers jostling each other on the nearby streets to get the best vantage point for showing their thumbs-up to their selfies. In summary: chaos.

Two of the largest firearm businesses with offices in the city offered drastic suggestions to put an immediate end to the problem—as long as a contract was forthcoming, of course. One of their proposals sent to Congress was for deploying an experimental weapon that sent out something similar to microwaves: they would cook the enemy, in this case the roaches, in a matter of seconds.

"And what about the cherry trees around the monument and the other flora and fauna along the river?" someone asked.

"Well," responded the CEO, "we'll take care of the main problem. Collateral effects are not our concern . . . they're secondary. We'll have to think about a second contract to cover the collateral damage."

The other corporation proposed placing a giant cover around the obelisk, like a giant, hermetically sealed bag, and then filling it with a poison gas to kill the insects in a matter of seconds . . . nothing experimental, something already tried and true.

"And what about the secondary effects of the gas?" someone else in the meeting asked. "What happens when you take the cover off?"

This CEO's answer was similar to the first corporate leader's, but he added the hope that the gases would be totally absorbed by the filthy insects. If not, they'd have to re-think the outcome, possibly replace the soil and grass around the obelisk and "vacuum" the place with a machine of some sort.

By dinnertime, the city was on pins and needles, focused on the operation to come. The eyes of the whole planet were placed on the obelisk, which seemed to have various layers of cockroaches. The roaches themselves were reproducing incredibly fast, feeding on each other ad infinitum. Some of the smallest ones began to move out toward the perimeter and were being smashed by men in HazMat suits wielding large flyswatters that were becoming more and more useless. Journalists were speculating, environmentalists developing theories and fatalists insisting it was a conspiracy. A religious extremist made his way through the crowds and began shouting through a megaphone about the end of the world and the seven plagues of Israel. By nightfall, the scene was darkening as no one could come to an agreement.

Martínez, who had not taken his eyes off the obelisk, said to himself, "Fuckin' scientists. Shouldn't the roaches have taken cover during the day? They're supposed to be hypersensitive to light and instinctively look for shade. Today they look like they're sunning themselves at the beach. It's incredible. . . ."

With the eyes of the world on the city he led, the mayor took advantage of the news, good and bad as it were, to press for an increase in the municipal budget and to lobby for the political and economic independence the city did not enjoy as the "federal district."

3

Various high-level meetings were called in Congress and at the White House. The chiefs of the armed services proposed launching a missile to finish off the invaders once and for all. Of course, that meant the destruction of the obelisk. At first, all were confounded by the proposal.

Someone at the conference table stood up and shouted, "Obliterate the obelisk?! . . . Unthinkable!"

The proposal's mastermind, a twelve-star general, took a long swig of coffee from his cup and calmly, somewhat dramatically, said, "Of course. We can always build another one. That's what we do in wartime. We blow it all up and then we put it back together again. Simple math: to rebuild is good. It generates profits, profits generate interest and that's the way of capitalism."

The eyes of a lobbyist representing the construction industry grew as big as saucers, and he added, "Seems to me that's a wonderful idea. That way, we can build an even bigger obelisk, twice as high. And that way, we can change the regulations on building heights in the city that are so restrictive and obsolete."

The assistant to the lobbyist, a very interesting kid from Harvard, took his boss' suggestion even further: "That way, the city can have taller buildings and change its looks . . . with modern skyscrapers."

Another associate of the lobbyist immediately stated that, once the obelisk was destroyed, it would facilitate the building of a giant bunker with various levels that would allow access to the Potomac River, the Metro and Rock Creek Park. The mouths of more than one of those present started to water at these proposals, and more than one politico thought about buying properties in the vicinity so they could be re-sold and torn down to make way for tall buildings and condos. In their mind's eyes they envisioned DC as a new New York City.

One of the old guard generals recommended using Napalm so as to burn those pests into crispy critters.

The meeting lasted almost until nightfall, with a variety of proposals on the table. While this had transpired, one of the insects emerged from the mass on one side of the obelisk and began to grow very large. And almost imperceptibly the other insects began to enter, one by one, the mouth of the larger roach, which continued to grow into immense proportions. Upon receiving reports of this, the armed forces chiefs met again and, thinking it the worst possible scenario, called in an infantry and an air force division. A state of siege was declared and all onlookers were removed from the area. The site was cordoned off and the press was prohibited. The soldiers evacuated Foggy Bottom and moved the residents into hotels around the city. As a national security precaution, all telecommunications and internet were being monitored and controlled. The president and vice president were escorted to secret bunkers for their own security and that of the nation. On the way, the president tweeted instructions stating, "Every single news report, every television camera shot must be censored and controlled, now that we are in a state of emergency and a possible attack."

"Is this a Trojan Horse, this time taking the form of a roach?" was a frequent question asked.

Running through the minds of alarmists were the Godzilla and King Kong movies, but instead of a giant ape they envisioned a giant roach flattening tanks, pulling jets from the sky and scattering the frightened population.

4

Before the night was over, for some two and a half hours, millions of roaches entered the mandible of the giant cockroach until not one more could fit. The soldiers, CIA officers and the national security forces stood in trepidation at the extraordinary sight. The thousands of police cars and Army vehicles seemed to shrink in size as the giant roach grew almost to the height of the obelisk itself. Suddenly the monster moved its head from side to side, rubbed its antennae and took two steps before falling to the ground on its back.

There was a soft murmur and even prayers from the crowd, suddenly followed by an outburst of weapons. Then a deadly silence followed. As spotlights shined over the insect, it started to move its legs and rock its body, trying to right itself like a turtle getting to its feet. But as quickly as it began it suddenly lay lifeless, like a tired, old fat man. The obelisk itself began to crack from its base to its peak. There were a couple of tense minutes. Then the giant roach looked around, opened its wings, stretched out its legs and became rigid. The soldiers, police and security personnel waited anxiously for

orders from their commanders, who expected the hellish insect to hop to its feet at any moment and attack everyone.

Fear permeated the city in silence, the macabre, rigid, brutal silence that had once overtaken Washington at the death
of Martin Luther King, Jr.

Then, to top it all off, the insect exploded into a million
tiny pieces, ". . . staining everything over a half mile around
the obelisk," as a journalist put it. What had rained down was
nothing more than millions of tiny, golden cockroaches that
scuttered into the sewers, cement cracks and niches over by
the Capitol building.

All stood in suspense, then disgust.

Some philosophers thought it all an omen of what was to
come; some intellectuals saw it as a metaphor for capitalism
and the politics of globalization. The construction company
representatives pounded the conference table in disappoint-
ment at having lost a great opportunity. The frustrated corporate munitions reps cursed the skies for having their plans
disrupted. Poets inspired by the happening drafted sad
prayers, and only the novelists, just the fiction writers, saw it
as more than just a symbol . . . as something else.

"Rot Is Stalking" was the banner headline the next day.

"We're Here and If You Get Rid of Us We'll Come Back"

for César Chávez

There are hundreds, thousands emerging from filthy kitchens, gardens, fields, under the rays of sun light, from the basements of rich folks, from the investment companies that traffic with the economy and politics . . . from everywhere.

"¡Aquí estamos y si nos echan regresamos!" they shout as they march forward.

"We come back because hunger is brutal, misery is ominous, poverty is horrible and economic disparity extreme. We're here, not to see the obelisk, row on the Potomac or visit the National Gallery. We're here to claim legal status, better treatment, a dignified life and a future for our children. The economic policies foisted on Latin America, the dirty wars, low-intensity warfare, the absence of democracy in our barren, conquered, beaten down, spied upon, sold, stateless administrations have created us."

They are here, and more are coming, emerging from the underground, shouting hoarsely in both English and Spanish: "Legalize us!" *"¡Reforma!"* "Stop Persecuting Immigrants . . ." *"Piedad . . ."*

9

Entire families holding hands, groups of women, friends all laughing and celebrating as if heading to a party. People and more people pouring out of Metro stations, joining the parade. Marching down every street, out of the shadows, with their children, their grandparents, aunts and uncles. They're all coming together: the twenty men who shared a two-room apartment or a dirty basement, those who were hidden in servants' quarters like slaves, as well as those who have come out with their sweethearts. They speak no English. The towns left behind had no schools, books, computers, just perhaps a church, a city hall and a small plaza of dried grass and skeletal trees.

They carry flags, drums, tambourines, rattles, and wear caps with their national colors. Their T-shirts read, "To be illegal is not criminal," "I contribute my work and my pay to the American economy," "An illegal is also a human being," "Say No to the Wall," "Down with the Wall" and "Latino Power!"

Respect.

They are the nameless ones, faceless, with false documents and whispers. They are the illegal finally out in the light of day and revealing their faces. They are us, and we are not alone, because we are supported by the usual suspects: students, teachers, leaders of various organizations that in Washington, DC, help the poor, the homeless and the undocumented. Then, of course, among them are undercover Migra agents secretly taking photos and videos, hiding behind sunglasses and in black sedans with tinted windows, communicating in code to each other.

"How many people are here marching, their footsteps echoing on the façades of government buildings? Where do they hide during the day? Where do they live? Who are they?" the onlookers ask themselves in wonder at the masses who have come out to march in protest in front of the US Congress. The spectators and tourists are at a loss for understanding.

"They're protesting? Well, aren't they illegal?"

Yes, all or most of them are undocumented. They're effort in getting here was costly, as was that of the Pilgrims. Crossing deserts, scaling the border wall, traveling for months in shipping containers and car trunks, in trailers transporting chickens, pigs or bananas. By plane, train, on foot and even underground in tunnels, who knows what else.

"Should it be a crime to escape hunger and exploitation?" a dark-skinned teenager explains to a reporter.

Traffic has been disrupted, horns are honking, sirens wailing, copters buzzing overhead, cops and more cops. A man is screaming out the window of his gray BMW as he is stymied by the traffic jam: "They should all be locked up and then sent packing back to their countries . . . ! Filthy pigs!"

A volley of whistles and hisses strikes back at him. "Fuck you!" someone shouts in perfect English.

That guy in the gray car doesn't know, I think, that all these people to my side, behind me and in front of me, for I can't imagine how many blocks, are the people who do the dirty work, not only in this city, but also for all of the entire US of A, cleaning restrooms and offices, slicing onions and meat in restaurants, harvesting crops in the southern states, assembling vehicles in midwestern factories, mixing cement at construction sites, stocking warehouse shelves, sewing textiles in basements and assembling electrical components in sweatshops. Yes, we're talking about hard work and heavy industry, the work no one else wants to do: cheap, dirty, poorly paid work under abusive conditions that make for illicit riches.

"We're here and if you get rid of us, we'll come back," echoes in a wave that envelops us all. I get goose bumps. There's no denying it's inspiring and catchy. Just like the music of Los Tigres del Norte, who play for this massive crowd they are part of.

We're surrounded by an army of police, who are directing traffic and blockading streets. I run into Mario, a smiley young man I met some five years ago at Casa de Maryland, an organization that helps immigrants.

"Hey, Mario, how you doin'?"

"Okay, I guess, you know, workin' . . . what else?"

We greet each other, chat for a while about our lives, and then he moves on just before we get to Constitution Avenue, where a group of lively Salvadorans joins the march, waving a large American flag. Mario is Guatemalan and can't return to his homeland because the same guys who killed his two brothers are out to get him for a petty offense during the civil war. He hasn't seen his mother in twenty years. He's got something wrong with his hearing but doesn't have health insurance, even while working eight hours a day, six days a week. He'd love to study to become an x-ray assistant but can't, he'd like to improve his English but doesn't have time to, he'd like to travel but is in mortal fear of being deported . . . like the rest of us, the thousands marching today in this capital city of this country built by immigrants.

We're passing in front of the Smithsonian now. It's the end of our march, but probably not the end of our movement—that's what they're calling it—given that as of today approximately a million of us have protested throughout the United States. The music of Los Tigres del Norte starts vibrating out of loudspeakers, with its accordion gasping wind in and out. A couple start dancing, then another. The evening falls gently as the multitudes begin to thin out and vanish discreetly, silently, as if by magic, into the shadows. . . . Within minutes, all are gone.

You Stopped for a Minute to Look around Me

for Roque Dalton

1

When you live in a foreign country, you're of no interest to anyone. No one asks you how you are, how's it going, and everyone avoids asking why you changed your life. Basically, no one asks because it's like small talk. You have a reason, and it has to be serious, vital. You're here because in your country there was nothing, at least nothing left for you. Most of the time, it's a question of money, although there are other reasons, some more powerful than others, but just as important. Maybe you had a house back in your homeland, some friends, a family, something more important, and that thing that makes all the rest of it understandable, just does not exist. That's why you're here, because of need, even at the expense of others, of other more personal reasons. You learn how to see things from a distance, and you start living in two places at the same time. Missing and comparing, and always holding on to two suitcases, ready to depart with each crisis, each grip of hunger, cold, loneliness, humiliation. We all know this, and that's why none of us asks. . . . Open secrets are best kept with sealed lips.

"I don't know about anyone else, but when I crossed over, I escaped the vicious cycle that had trapped me."

2

You had a life back there, a life that doesn't look anything like what you're living today, because now you have no one. The worst is on Sundays, when the sun beats down on your apartment walls, and like a mop dripping dirty water you head out to the street full of noise and people, but none of them are yours.

What to do? Where to go? Rent a movie cassette? Go to the supermarket to buy groceries? Get into a car and escape at full speed? Or walk around the traffic circle, the block, back to the fuckin' place where you landed a few years ago that still is not yours? Well, you keep walking, alone, like a stray dog. And you learn to appreciate a passing smile, a greeting however cold it may seem.

3

In retrospect, you know that change is painful. You don't have close friends. You're surrounded by people who don't know you, and you don't really know them either. You're like a phantom, and you handle your relationships with kid gloves so as not to leave fingerprints. You have two sets of ID, a Social Security number that belongs to a dead person. You're one of many others in the same situation—everybody knows it and participates in the conspiracy. We're undercover in a conspiracy of silence. We're afraid, in the dark, working in obscurity. . . . You are one with the many others, without knowing each other. You successfully escaped the violence that stayed behind the border wall. You are among the poorly paid people struggling for bread, doing the lousy jobs that weren't

available in your homeland. You are the cheap labor that sup-
ports this country, despite what the brainless citizens think as
they threaten us with lynching, as in the old times.

We're poor, for sure, but ultimately we're people with
dreams and aspirations. We produce what's bought and consumed by the population from day to day, yes, leaving a piece
of our liver in the furniture we craft, a kidney and a lung in the
clothes that are worn, eyes and hands in the produce that is
eaten, other body parts in luxury cars driving down roads, in
the dancing shoes . . . everything that surrounds us, complete
bodies. . . . Products without our fingerprints, very few.

4

"One year doesn't end before we find ourselves in a new
one. That's life, confusing. There's always something that
needs to be done, but gets interrupted, crossed off. More than
anything, work, making a living, is the priority. Even though
I feel the same, I know I'm not the same person."

You shake your head, trying to rid yourself of those
thoughts. Over here, people call it depression and swallow
pills to live happily in an artificial paradise. And then you
think, how fast time has gone by since you began this life as a
chauffeur behind the wheel and learned the names of so many
highways. And how time flies before you can get to the mem-
oir you'd like to write, when you finally can vanquish the language barrier. You spy an eagle on the horizon, flying
elegantly across the sky to the mountains. You slow down to
look around, with fresh eyes, yes, as if it is all new to you, even
though it's already been twenty of forty-two years of your life.
Years of hard work, not only as a chauffeur, but also working
in the fields, in kitchens, in office buildings scrubbing toilets.
You ask yourself, then, have you succeeded? Once again you

remember how you were when you crossed at Laredo, a young man from El Salvador seeking to forge his future. Your father had been murdered because he would not turn over his salary to a bunch of lowlifes, your poor old mother living in a hovel of two tiny rooms—although it did have a cement floor and a tin roof, a television and a gas stove.

As your car idles at an intersection, you consider how much you'd like to rewind the movie reel, put the car in reverse gear at that intersection and travel backwards in time . . . return to when you were happy for a few hours, minutes, seconds. You smile at the possibility of seeing your movie again, this time in the land of opportunity: the dinner table covered in food, a smiling father, a proud mother, a country without poverty, without corruption. . . . Damn, you say to yourself, why is happiness always envisioned as something in the past? You look into the rearview mirror: there's no one on that highway who can split the desert in two. Then you realize that rewinding the movie has its risks. You know it: it's that foul taste in your mouth, the tears that are now flowing down your cheeks.

You took this road in order to forget, even if at times you can't.

You look at your watch, at the sun on the horizon, you're late again.

Work Abandoned

for Luis Buñuel

Carlos Villegas rested the mattress for a minute on the tip of his shoes so that it would not get dirty while he waited for the traffic light to turn red so that he could cross. He stood at the corner of Independencia and Revolución, right in front of the Exporte department store, where he had worked as a young man. The traffic stopped to let the pedestrians cross, and he once again hoisted the double mattress onto his back. He crossed the avenue in front of a parade of people who were like shadows on their way to work or returning home from the night shift. Villegas let an aged woman pass him who was loaded down with supermarket bags sealed with tape. He crossed the street with his mattress like Sisyphus and his boulder. Following behind him were his two children and their burdens: Jimena with a box of kitchen utensils and Anselmo with big bundle of clothes wrapped in a bedsheet. It was the fourth time that day that they trudged to their new home, with two more trips remaining. Anselmo kept his eyes to the ground, embarrassed that anyone would see him; he was also attempting to block out the street sounds that were drilling into his ears.

They walked three blocks and then started up a dirt road
to the top of a mountain and to the top floor of the Brisas del
Norte (Northern Breezes) complex, which from a distance
looked like a boat docked in the desert. Under that preten-
tious name the unfinished apartment complex had been proclaimed six years earlier as the architectural wonder of the
decade. Carlos Villegas still remembered the first time he saw
the sign in the courtyard of the state government building and
heard Governor Aparicio Moctezuma and his Chief of Public Works Donaldo Cervantes announce: "From Brisas del
Norte not only will people be proud to have the precious vista
before their very eyes of the sister city of Laredo, but they'll
also be able to have a comfortable, spacious and first-world
lifestyle." This was followed by applause, toasts, the laying of
the corner stone, *abrazos*, photos for the press of the governor
with a shovel full of sand, speeches glorifying economic de-
velopment and progress.

Now, six years after the euphoric speeches, what was left
was the smallest project of the century with various buildings
abandoned and others half built. There were now hundreds
of families made homeless and poor.

Carlos Villegas once again took a breather, this time by
leaning on a car bumper, before heading up the mountain
path, which was a short cut that would save him at least a kilo-
meter, via the curves and field in front of Brisas, his new
home. . . . "A new house," he liked to boast to his friends when
he still took pride in paying the mortgage monthly. He had
invested his life's savings at the top of that arid mountain, and
that included the money from the sale of his car and what he
had inherited from his father, Don Rafael. He took a deep
breath and cursed his imbecile self. He knew he had been sold
a bill of goods, tricked, humiliated and, worse, his miscalcu-

lations had made him look naïve to the two people following him in the heat of that day.

"A lot of dust does not make for good land." He could still hear the wisdom of his father's words.

It was less than eight months earlier that Governor Aparicio Moctezuma swore repeatedly that he'd finish the Brisas project. At one press conference he stated, "This project has personal meaning for me: the pride of my administration." That very same day, Public Works Chief Cervantes led an army of workers and machinery to the small mountain to start the third stage of the residential portion of the project. Once again, there was applause, praise and more photos in the newspapers. Within a few days, the future residents rushed to the banks to make their mortgage payments. The cost of naiveté was enormous for Carlos; not only had he taken a loan out on his shoe repair shop, but eventually it led to its loss.

Villegas had no idea how that had happened. For three years the only topic of conversation had been the new apartment with its three bedrooms, living room, dining room, two bathrooms, the panoramic view from the seventh floor and the two parking spaces below.

"You'll see, honey, how things will all be better . . . and most important, the kids will each have their own bedrooms," he'd repeat to his wife every time she complained about skimping to save for the new place.

Now, stark reality had confirmed her fears, and Carlos felt even more guilt.

The first part of the project to be finished was a group of buildings that faced a classy residential zone in Laredo. On its completion, the governor threw a party for the members of his cabinet and invited his counterpart on the Texas side of the wall to be photographed together with their families in front of the finished buildings. Carlos returned home that evening very excited. He trusted the governor, he had faith in the projected plans for a new life, a better and more beautiful one. That the authorities were already celebrating confirmed that all was going as planned and that, even better, they were ahead of schedule. The photo in the newspaper of the governor holding hands with his children in front of the finished buildings gave the investors even more hope. In the following moths of making the down payment and then just a month after the governor passed his office to his associate Lucio Guerra—by means of electoral fraud, of course—the first signs of trouble appeared. A journalist for *El Norte* had uncovered the farce. Within one week, the hopes and dreams of Carlos crashed into the unsavory truth. The reporter had been able to sneak past the guards and barbed-wire fences to discover that they were only running the motors of machinery, not actually working, and the construction workers were only digging holes and later filling them in. There were no construction materials, architects nor funds to continue the work. The scandal was covered in eight front-page columns of *El Norte*. Carlos broke out in a cold sweat and was on the verge of passing out. *How could such a bold-faced fraud happen?*

Carlos took a moment to rest against a pole at the corner bus stop. That was the last straw: he had thrown his life's savings out the window. *How could I have trusted that man . . . ?* Everyone now knew that the governor had relocated to Europe with Miss Tamaulipas and would probably end up in the Solomon or the Canary Islands. It was all a sad joke. He raised his eyes to the heavens, where Public Works Chief Cervantes was in a plane headed in another direction. Beside him sat his wife with her hair bleached blond, wearing dark sunglasses; behind them sat their blond children. According to *El Norte*, the fraud began with Cervantes selling the land to the Bienestar construction company, one of the many shell companies that had been created during Moctezuma's six-year term.

The newspaper had enumerated the extensive list of laws broken by the governor and his cohorts: "The fraudulent sale of public lands, bribery, forged licenses and counterfeit documents, laundering funds, drug trafficking, cover-ups, collecting non-existent taxes, misappropriation of funds . . ." More than that, there was nepotism, lying to the voters, leaving working-class families penniless, all facilitated by violating human and civil rights, all under the guise of enforcing the law and the constitution.

Hundreds of kilometers away, Moctezuma was lifting his fourth flute of champagne and toasting the beautiful and just as ambitious Rocío Vergara, Miss Tamaulipas. She leaned forward and kissed him on the lips. Out the aircraft window, they could see all the way to the horizon, their happy ending.

Once again Carlos rested their twenty-five-year old mattress on the tips of his shoes. He was just about seventy meters from the Brisas del Norte residential units. He tried to focus his eyes and squinted. For some strange reason he could not focus; it was like trying to see a boat in a fog bank. He had been at that same spot some three times that morning and he could almost swear that what he spied was a mirage emerging from the arid floor of the desert, or a cardboard backdrop erected for a low-budget film, not even stage scenery, not even a half-constructed frame. "A gym, so that the young people don't get into drugs," Moctezuma had proclaimed proudly. As for the Olympic-size pool, there was only a large pit in the ground with very few studs placed, and around it hundreds of little piles of sand, gravel and limestone, along with some stacks of red brick. Only two buildings had been completed— that is, their exterior, given that inside they were missing bathroom fixtures, electric switches and doors. Two poor-quality concrete buildings faced Laredo, which in contrast looked impressive. The floors of the two elephantine buildings had to be reached on foot, given that they were missing elevators and emergency exits. The two giant box structures exhibited attractive, well-designed façades, which could only be appreciated as seen from the other side of the border wall, but in reality the buildings were like besieged medieval castles emerging from the fog of war. *Like a city squashed by the foot of a giant*, was the only way Carlos could describe the image before his eyes, although thousands of words crowded his mind.

Now, Carlos would have to go work on the other side of the wall, like hundreds of others, to labor as a dishwasher, janitor, gardener or kitchen helper . . . to put up with mistreatment by the Gringos and their haughty, arrogant, prejudicial perspectives. "Perspective," was another term he remembered from Moctezuma's speeches. *How is it possible?* Maybe on that count, architect Cervantes was correct. He was a graduate of Monterrey Tech, with a masters from Yale and a doctorate from Harvard, where for sure he had met his *compadre* Aparicio. "Perspective, where art and daily life coincide . . ." "Perspective" echoed in Carlos' mind like a coin falling through the slot on a piggy bank. "Perspective" slipped from his lips like a magic word, and in his articulation he discharged all of the powerlessness he felt and that was sweating out his pores. "Perspective," the word was now diluted as if it had bounced down the steps of a pyramid. He repeated the word once more and wanted to shout it, dislodging it once and for all from his gullet, letting it explode from his lungs, from his heart; he wanted to throw it against the godforsaken scenery that faced him, out of focus and blurry. It was a house of cards about to be tumbled down by all the people who had been defrauded by institutions that would never be held to account . . . time and time again. . . . *How long will this go on?* he asked himself. Ironically, "perspective" was what that infamous group of unfinished buildings had in common. Of course, without the promised statues, trees, kiosks and green areas planned for the end of the governor's term.

Carlos squeezed the mattress upon remembering the damn prospectus for the project that encouraged him to invest in the scam like someone placing the hangman's noose around his own neck. *What an imbecile; that's how I'll be remembered.* If and when he worked on the other side of the wall, maybe at a Chinese restaurant, and looked across at that gorgeous façade, it would confirm that he had been the poor devil responsible for his family getting fucked. He felt like crying but knew that too would only confirm his defeat, so he held it in. He would not cry, ever . . . although he expected that on arriving at his "new home" he'd feel the urge again. A bare apartment with bare walls of cinder block outlined with cement mortar. As bare as a wound: grey rooms without floors, doors, and with two holes in the wall for bathroom fixtures. For lighting, a metal box without wires to connect anything. From where he stood, the project was a half-erected city made up of four towers that looked like poorly located wooden crates covered in flagstone, a flattened city that he predicted would be a ghost town in less than a year, if it lasted that long. A city without city services and without children. Like a pink merengue cake poorly baked, with a savage bitemark on its side. Plastic sheets covering the windows, canvas sheets covering doorways as in refugee camps. Not a home but a shelter, a mouse hole. It would serve as proof for the rest of his life that he had been scammed, taken advantage of, paying for a house and receiving a cell.

That's what aggravated him the most, to know that he had paid in gold and gotten shit, as had warned his wife and his brother-in-law had warned, who now despised him, especially because his two children's plans for attending university were now tenuous. Carlos felt the hate was flushing his face hot and he loosened his grip for a moment so as not to explode. He wiped the sweat from his brow . . . he still could not believe what was happening to him.

"Hurry up, dammit!" he yelled at his children, who were yards behind him with their loads. They stared back at him with more wonder than rancor. The three of them looked like a trio of thieves in the middle of the desert some fifty, one hundred, two hundred years back. Three absurd characters forced to carry junk, arriving at the entrails of what once was a large fish named Moby Dick or a sunken ship. Carlos closed his eyes and took in the light breeze that refreshed him for a moment, despite it smelling of French fries, roasted meat and ketchup. To him it also reeked of poison, disrespect, illusion. Again he breathed in, filling his lungs with the breeze, and he relaxed the tensed muscles on his arms a bit. For just a second, he let go of the mattress, and that pleasant breeze knocked it over with unsuspecting force, pushing him down to the ground as well. Dazed at first, he then realized what had happened as he spotted the mattress rolling away like a square tire. He looked at his kids, searched their eyes, but only saw them following their parents' mattress literally gone with the wind. They could not decide whether to laugh or cry. Carlos was in shock, terrified, and took off running desperately after the mattress, which was rolling faster and faster down the hill he had climbed. He ran as fast as his legs would carry him. He just could not afford to lose the mattress, their bed; he couldn't let them even take away even the bed they slept in, the bed in which he begat his children, who were the only positive things in his life.

"No!!!" a blood-curdling scream issued from deep within. No, he would not let that northerly breeze . . . no, never.

The Labyrinth

for Octavio Paz

I dreamt I was in a labyrinth. I was pursued by the mythical *chingada,* the violated woman, fat, with enormous tits, smiling with rotten teeth. I had no idea why she was coming after me, maybe to fuck me. I went down another of the paths of the labyrinth whose walls were made of garbage, where starving children were digging into mounds of detritus. I started running in zigzags to avoid others who were there begging for change. Adrenaline was pumping through my heart as I opened my eyes wide looking for an exit, but there was none I could see through the smoke of something burning and the very tall walls. I paused for a second to catch my breath. I noticed that the children could not see me, their eyes like pale mollusks were without pupils.

The *chingada,* the violated woman, began wailing, lifted her arms to grab me. I started running again and taking great leaps forward. I turned into a curve in that strange place whose stench was overwhelming. There were insects climbing all over the stacks of waste, rodents and other creatures trying to survive in that place. The most disconcerting part was that the floor down the alleyway I was using to escape that terrifying being was clean, made up of a fine white sand from some Caribbean beach. The walls on each side seemed to have a strange texture, with protruding milk cartons, old soup cans and packaging for frozen food, products for babies, grand-parents and young people, total detritus. Without slowing down, I turned to look at the predator at my heels. Her three tits were swinging left and right, and the strands of her straight, filthy hair were like dark, writhing serpents. In some places, the path abruptly turned into corners, at other places long curving corridors. For an instant I thought about climb-ing up one of those walls. I tried it and the garbage tumbled down, almost burying me. I got to my feet fast on hearing the thumping paces of the *chingada*, who was pounding the ground and charging like a bull. I remember arriving at an in-tersection of paths where I had already run and stopped to catch my breath. The female monster also stopped, but only for a second and then almost caught me. I remember think-ing, What's the sense in running, trying to escape in this cir-cular world? Why not confront my destiny?

That's when I woke up—perhaps a changed person, but for sure with a different perspective on things—in front of a locked door and a wall so high it reached the sky. On the other side was desolation, the desert . . . I thought of my brothers and sisters.

"I hope my family is okay," I said, and I got goose bumps.

Once You're Down, Don't Forget to Ask for God's Help

for the Chicano activists, teachers and artists and their legacy

It was a strange scene, especially for the first of the month—and a Monday. The guy was screaming at God with all his might, looking up to the skies above the skyscrapers in desperation. I looked up. Maybe the two of us below looked like insignificant scratches on the ground, dots moving from one place to another, to the people in the windows at the top of those buildings. Really insignificant.

We were at Times Square, the greatest commercial symbol in the world, after Tokyo that is. It's the must-see square that divides Manhattan in two.

"Hey, God! Are you there?!" he yelled again, full throated. He kept swiveling his head as he looked up, totally ignored by the thousands and thousands of windows above and by the clouds above the skyscrapers.

I was the only passerby to stop and observe him.

"Hey, God, are you listening?" he shouted to the four winds.

He didn't look like a homeless guy, or crazy, or one of the thousands of unhinged inhabitants of this city, in which almost everyone has mental health issues. He was dressed in a navy-blue suit, light-blue shirt and striped tie, but was wearing slippers without socks.

He started shouting again, his face red from the strain, now begging: "God, are you there?! Answer me, damn it!" His eyes were wide open.

I didn't know if he truly expected his shouts to reach the heavens, but the truth is they never even got beyond the sidewalk, what with all the noise on New York streets: cars and trucks honking, people shouting into cellphones, jets flying overhead, machines vibrating, the noise of everything in motion.

The guy was totally ignored, or avoided as crazy man.

I looked him over carefully and tried to imagine his life. He didn't seem dirty. He could be a scientist, a clergyman or a history teacher. What could have driven him to this? Maybe he just lost his mind all of a sudden on his way to carry out his daily routine, which is entirely possible—it could happen to anyone. Right?

I headed for the corner. It was getting late.

And then I saw the man cross the street in a group of pedestrians, like a normal person. Although once he was on the other sidewalk, he stopped and looked up and shouted to God as loud as he could, once again searching earnestly beyond the skyscrapers for God to appear. He blasted out another frustrated shriek, this time calling for the "Lord." He stuck his hands into his pockets and walked up to the street corner, and then crossed the street back to the corner he had occupied ten minutes earlier. He slowly dragged his feet in my direction, then stopped halfway and howled again at the heavens with his eyes full of hope in total disregard of all the passersby as he concentrated on his mission.

I searched in my jacket pocket for a couple of dollar bills as I walked toward the subway entrance. Before plunging down the stairway, I too turned my eyes up to the sky in hope . . . just in case God was to answer him. . . . And if He did, maybe God would see me too, if only for a few seconds.

A Bar Scene Somewhere on the Map

for José Agustín

Ross was downing a cheap, greasy meal and having a beer at some joint on the highway. There was a female truck driver seated at the end of the bar—thirty and pretty tall and well built and apparently intimidating to many a guy. She too was eating while watching the football game on the TV.

Yes, Ross thought to himself and smiled, he was attracted to big women, even if they pounded him. The bottle blond had no class apparently, picking her nose a couple of times, scratching her armpit and eating with her hands, although none of that lessened her beauty and strong body, which she carried with masculine disregard.

After finishing her chicken wings and coleslaw, she turned to look at him, sensing she had been observed. At first, he had thought she was a lesbian, but soon realized his mistake. Rather, it looked like she was waiting for him. And after downing a third beer, she came over to sit next to Ross, seeing there was no action from him.

"Shit, we're the only two people in this joint, and there's so much wasted space, don't ya think?" she said as she sat down next to him.

"Yeah, I'll drink to that," he said, smiling and extending his hand. "I'm Anthony Ross, it's a pleasure."

"Nice ta meetcha, I'm Jana."

Ross felt her calloused hands and the strength of her grip.

"To your health," Ross said and couldn't resist looking her over: legs, breasts, hips.

"What brings you here, Anthony?"

"I'm on my way to Lubbock. How about you?" Ross asked without resisting another look at her thighs and waist.

She looked at him with indifference, although she noticed the once-over he had given her.

"I'm taking a load of Japanese motors to Baltimore, but I can't get in until Monday."

"Is there some regulation?"

"Many."

"I see."

"It's a holiday weekend and there are specific regs . . . besides there'll be a lot of traffic, a real nightmare."

"How much of a delay? A couple of hours to get downtown?"

"Two? I wish. . . . Four or five just sitting in fuckin' traffic, burnin' gas," Jana said.

"Yeah, it's better to spend the cash on a drink than on gas," he kidded.

"Yeah, I agree."

He turned and asked the bartender for two beers, one for himself and one for his "friend."

"In a day and a half, all I've gotta do is get on the Interstate and it's a clear shot from here until I deliver the goods at 8 am on Monday. The worst traffic is at 10."

"Yeah, that's smart; you decided to take the afternoon off."

"Why not?"

"Five hours of traffic is too much for me too," Ross agreed.

"I know about traffic, believe you me," she said wide-eyed.

They both laughed.

The barman placed the beers in front of them.

"How long have you been at this gig?" Ross asked as he raised the beer bottle to his lips.

"It's goin' on six years."

"Well, then, you're an expert."

"But I prefer havin' a beer in a cantina," the trucker said.

They both laughed again.

"To your health."

A reporter on the TV was interviewing the inventor of the Selfiearm, which was nothing more than a tripod and a device to grip the cellphone, the "genius" explained.

"According to statistics, the people who take the most selfies are ugly-looking," Ross commented like some trivia expert.

"Really?" Jana turned to look at him, suddenly interested.

"That's why the internet is flooded with ugly faces these days."

They both laughed at the unkind comment and signaled the barman, as they were really into their beers now.

"Since no one ever took photos of them before, the uglies are doing it themselves now."

"They're recording themselves for posterity, they think."

"They think?"

They laughed again.

"We humans are pretty cruel, don't you think?" Jana said.

Just then Ross noticed a feminine gesture in his new friend. He liked her, especially her dark, enigmatic eyes, besides that stunning body, of course.

"Yeah, we're really cruel."

"Ya think we were born that way?"

"That's not what they say, you know . . . we learn by imitation. From the time a child is born it imitates the adults."

They both looked at the TV screen and thought about it for about ten minutes, sipping their beers, Ross' dark and Jana's light.

"When you said that, something occurred to me."

"What's that?"

"I'm from the South, 'n down there we respect social class lines. At the top of the heap are the high-sounding last names. At the bottom are the rednecks, blacks and Latins, in that order."

"I see."

"I belong to the first group. . . . So be careful what you say," she warned him, gesturing with her index finger.

"I didn't say anything," Ross said, holding up his hands.

"I was raised on a ranch," she continued. "What happened was that all the guys at the bottom of the heap on that wealthy ranch were after the two daughters of the wetback Mexican maid . . . both the blacks and the rednecks abused them. Believe it or not, the poor girls were nicknamed 'baldy' because of something unfortunate that happened. They'd gotten a headful of lice, and those bugs jumped from their heads unto the hair of the boss' grandmother, and from there onto an aunt who lost a bunch o' hair right before an important shindig they were gonna have. She got so angry that she went to the maid's room and took shears to the girls' hair. That's where they got their nickname. They were treated like shit. They went around hairless for about ten years . . . until one day they just disappeared. No one knew if the INS grabbed them or if they just left town."

Ross shook his head. "Don't you feel sorry for them?"

"Sure, but I was just a girl at the time, and it wasn't my fault."

Ross shook his head again. "It's just cowards that think they can abuse the weak, that makes 'em feel more manly," he said like he meant it.

Jana took a big swallow of her beer and said, "Not just men, I know a lot of abusive women. I agree with you, buddy, only cowards bask in their manliness by abusing the defenseless, including women and unarmed people."

The commercials had run their course on the TV, and the football game continued.

Ross didn't give a damn about either team, but he did enjoy seeing how the plays took shape, especially defensive strategies.

"You're gonna think I'm crazy," Jana said, glassy-eyed, "but I learn the most in bars, hotels, casinos and gas stations."

"Yeah, I can understand that."

Just at that moment a man came in and stepped up to the bar. He sat down next to Jana, ordered a tequila and a beer. The bartender came right back with the order promptly and placed it in front of his third client. The newcomer picked up his shot and toasted the couple.

Everyone echoed the toast, including the bartender, who served himself white rum with water.

"To your health," they said in unison.

"In this culture," the newcomer started, "hunting is a solitary act. You're given a rifle, and you can patiently spend a day or a month, but you can't go home until you're covered in blood and you've got something to show for it."

Ross felt the guy's comment was out of place. Jana didn't respond to it either. The man emptied his glass and ordered another shot.

Again the bartender served him his drink in a timely manner.

"Words of wisdom should be placed in jars and closed tight so that they don't stink. They're like embryos, catalogued and shelved in secret. Some people collect them, but the politicians tend to make them disappear, although some keep the jars in the lower drawers of their expensive desks. You need to take the air out of truth so that it doesn't mildew and rot. Like everything else, truth has a life cycle. Sometimes it changes color and many other times, especially when it's combined in the same jar, some of the truths separate like oil and water—those are the lies. The unborn truths are the ones the politicians try to hide, like monsters with pig tails, three eyes, stunted limbs and eight toes on their feet."

Ross took the guy for either a poet or an inspired drunk.

"There are three types of equilibrium according to science: stable equilibrium, unstable equilibrium and neutral equilibrium. The location of the center of gravity is of the greatest importance in determining equilibrium and the stability of a body. When a body returns to its original position, after having been displaced, it's said to be stable."

Then the guy got up, left cash on the bar and left the way he had entered the place. Once Jana and Ross were alone again, they broke into loud guffaws.

Sitting at the bar, Ross realized in his drunk stupor how random life is and how useless existence is.

"The first time I shot at someone," Ross began, "I felt sad more than anything, as if I had lost something, I don't know what. I felt like I had a knot in my throat for a few days and a slight heartache. To feel better about it, I had to keep telling myself that the man was an assassin, a bad person, not good but someone who deserved it because he was a danger to other people and he'd continue to do damage and create pain. It nevertheless was still hard."

Ross' words left Jana cold. She readjusted in her seat, without knowing—she'd find out later during their intimacy—that to many in the system of justice system, the man sitting beside her was a legend: a paid assassin.

Road Movie

---

for my father (1942-2017)

1

The eight-cylinder red sports car stopped, and a man no older than thirty years old got out and slammed the door shut. He looked into the distance, then walked up to a fence with a "No Trespassing" sign. The barrier seemed endless in both directions. There was a large lock on a chain strung between metal posts. He took a drag on his cigarette and looked into the distance: the road extended the length of that stupid barrier. It was a beautiful highway that crossed the Chihuahuan desert. He pulled off his glasses, crushed his cigarette underfoot and thought about the situation. He didn't want to return.

He pressed the clutch and put the car into reverse. The car backed up some twenty meters and stopped. It had been quiet up to then, but he pushed a button on the console and slid a cassette in. A litany of electric guitars screeched like thousands of glass panes fracturing. He pushed the gas pedal all the way to the floor and car wheels spun out in shrieks. He heard himself cry out and closed his eyes for a second upon feeling the impact. He gripped the steering wheel, hearing the bang as the car flew into the air and touched down.

The driver opened his eyes and braked. The Corvette skidded in the soft sand of the road's shoulder. He took in a deep breath and got out of the car again to assess the damage. Just a dent in the trunk, a small dent in the bumper and two large scratches on the left side. *To hell with the border,* he uttered. He slapped the car door and got back in. He picked up his cigarette pack from the dashboard and lit one. Morning light was beginning to shine in the distance, and soon the unforgiving sun of the desert would be up.

He pressed the clutch and burned rubber.

It was the beginning of a true American story. It was as it should be: a desolate highway bordered by cactus, mirages and a sun-bleached bull skull on an anthill. He took a deep drag from his cigarette and blew smoke rings at the rearview mirror. Cigarettes, warm beer, peanuts and fast food was all he had eaten in the last few days. Behind him red clouds, before him the horizon. He put it in fifth gear and put his glasses into their case. The motor was humming—he loved that sound. He loved the feeling of freedom, the wind in his face, nothing but the highway and the median line ahead. He turned down the volume and began tapping his fingers on the steering wheel. He liked the song and began to sing along. He was enjoying the unending pleasure of asphalt, the white line trying to escape his eight powerful cylinders that were tearing up the ground against time and distance.

What was the meaning of that red race car crossing a picturesque oasis of cactus and dry grass?

Peter smiled with the knowledge that he'd find Valeria. He hit a button on the eight-track and the song started over. The engine's roar was louder now, vibrating the air, disturbing the peace of the desert. The metal beast and its driver were forcing rodents back into their lairs, awakening coiled snakes from their sunbaths and causing lizards to change color on the sandy background. The roar of the red beast also made the vultures and other scavengers nervous.

The desert, as seen through a drop of cactus liquid, the desert, where hardly anything happens except for daily tragedy where once there was a valley, a sea, a lagoon, fields; the desert, symbol of nothingness. Arizona as far as you can see, night turning into day, the recently red sky turning pale blue, the Corvette's headlights still beaming.

Such was the ideal image of the lone venturer, although for him it was more than the role in a play he was condemned to portray. Photographed from in front, then from the side, the wheels spinning, a hand gripping the steering wheel, a cowboy boot pushing the accelerator down, the landscape reflected in the driver's sunglasses, the remains of a cigarette butt in the ashtray. . . . The radio speakers vibrating with wild music as the needle rises on the speedometer. The rearview mirror escaping the shrinking highway. Guitar music cutting through the silence and the static air.

It was an American cliché, he thought: the story of a man hurtling towards his destiny in this unique panorama laid out before him. Ridiculous. Really, to try one's luck in the desert? He smiled to himself.

Overhead that great fountain of light, the sun, was racing its way to noon for the second day in a row. It was like a fiery racing car enveloped in a halo and the real smell of burnt rubber pervaded the movie set. In this scenario his car sported an aerodynamic design, with carburetors firing fuel like a machine gun. In the distance, Peter could see a town. He pressed the clutch and put it in fourth gear as the car slid around a curve. In front, the countryside rushed by as the mountains receded behind him. Up came a sign announcing gas and lodging, and he looked at the gas gauge—less than half a tank. He'd take a nap before gassing up.

He yawned. It was okay to sleep a while, to rest. He'd spent a day and a night on the road, driving without a stop. He flipped the directional and lifted his foot off the gas to take another curve. "Flagstaff," a sign announced. He slowed down and stopped at a red light. He was on the outskirts of the city and could read a sign in the distance: "Canyon City Motel." His eyelids felt like a metal curtain drawing down over a storefront entrance. He headed into the motel driveway and parked beside a horse-transport trailer. He turned off the engine and waited for the dust he'd raised to clear. He extracted the cassette from the player and turned the console off, got out of the Corvette, stretched his arms, lifted his feet and headed for the motel office. He registered as Peter Wimbert, although his real name was Peter García.

The desk clerk was listening to country music and paging through a porn magazine on the counter. Peter paid, walked down the corridor with a key and just then remembered he had to phone someone, although he could not remember whom. He was just too tired to think. Dead tired. He got to his room on automatic pilot and entered. He quickly turned on the TV with the volume lowered, sat down on the bed, took off his shoes, fell back and slept for two whole days.

Car lights emerged from the curve in the road, the race car took flight from the pavement for about ten seconds, softly returned to earth and disappeared in the shadows. From down the road apiece came the smell of burnt tires and steaming gasoline in a race against time.

2

Peter García had left San Antonio some three months earlier. His father had died, and on a whim left his son the car he was driving now. His father had kept it impeccable, cherry.

Beyond the car, there was nothing else: no house of course, no sense of belonging to a town or city, no other relatives except for a couple of distant uncles on his father's side who supposedly lived in the city he was headed for in the middle of the desert. On his mother's side there were still some living relatives in New Mexico; he had rarely visited them and probably would never see them again. Peter had spent his entire childhood in mobile homes, trailer parks, vans and hotel rooms. It wasn't until he was fourteen that his parents decided to settle down and send their son to school. "The road is no place for a child, the boy needs roots," his mother was convinced. His father, on the other hand, was saddened to miss temporary home addresses, halftime jobs and passing friendships. They decided to stay in Asheville, not because the schools were good or because rent was cheap but because that's where their two-room camper bit the dust after 90,000 miles. With the few bucks from the sale of the camper on top of some scant savings, they were able to make a down payment on a small mobile home with a garden and a car port, and that's where Peter lived for the next twelve years, where he spent his teenage years and where his parents grew old and died. In the end, the pretty little mobile home was lost, as was the small laundry his mother managed until she became ill with cancer. Time leaves no survivors.

Peter woke up hungry. His stomach growled as he got out of bed. He looked into the mirror and saw how thin and dirty he was. He took a whiff of his stinky armpits, he also could smell his malodorous feet. He remembered he had dreamed, it was always the same thing: some brave guy crashes his car through a metal door set right in the middle of a lonely highway.

He bathed and, with no clean clothes at hand, put on what he had been wearing, except for the socks, which were

43

bunched up in the corner by the commode. He left the room and went to the front desk to pay for another day. Then he went to his car and, before starting the engine, put on a pair of socks he kept in the glove compartment. He got out of the car and lifted the hood, took out the dipstick to check the oil. It was fine, so was the water, the antifreeze and the brake fluid. Back in the car, he put it in reverse and reminded himself he needed gas. He felt like having a cheeseburger and fries. He'd eat breakfast on the way.

He had gotten it into his head to bring the news of his father's demise to his two uncles. It was the least he should do. While waiting for the gas pump to reach finish up, he examined the map of Arizona. According to his calculations, it wouldn't take more than a day and a half to reach his destination. Once the tank filled, he went in to pay. He bought five bottles of water, a twelve-pack of beer, two giant bags of potato chips, a package of peanuts and cigarettes. He scarfed down two hot dogs while the clerk was packing his purchases in plastic bags. He also picked up two cans of oil and one of antifreeze. Maybe he should wait until nightfall to travel, he re-considered, since the temperature was supposed to reach beyond 120 degrees, although night travel also its own risks.

While he was paying, a pretty redhead entered and smiled at him. He smiled back and winked at her. He took his change, shoved it into his pants pocket and turned to face the rear of the store. She was searching through the refrigerated cases. Nice body, he decided.

He returned to his car, still retaining the young woman's image in his mind. He turned on the radio and the AC, but not the motor. He flipped open a beer and gulped down more than half the can, then belched. He opened a bag of chips and grabbed a handful. He chewed slowly, downed the rest of the beer and dropped the can into the plastic bag. Finally she stepped out the door and ran to a truck hauling horses. He recognized the vehicle. It was the same one he had seen in the parking lot of the motel that first day. The driver was another woman, older, with black hair and very pale skin. Her mother?

Are they from a ranch around here? As the truck turned the corner, Peter turned on the ignition. He was sure he'd run into them again. He smiled to himself. He liked her . . . in fact, he thought he'd seen her somewhere before.

He headed down the secondary road shown on the map laying on the passenger seat.

Of course all of what I'm relating here took place before the existence of cellphones and GPS. How much before? Somewhat, as you can see by the characters' clothes, the material objects and the car models. The main guy is passing through the past, although he is not completely from there.

3

Peter came to a dead stop. Enough already, he was lost. Now he'd have to backtrack at least twenty-five miles to get his bearings. He looked at the map again. He must have gone wrong taking the highway to the south instead of the north. He shook his head, made a U-turn and drove down the same highway he'd just travelled, cursing himself. As he drove by a stretch of curves, he noticed a horse trailer stopped on the shoulder. He passed it up and in his rearview saw the two women bent over the truck engine that must have stalled. He stopped. In his rearview he also examined the young woman's body: good hips, long, well-shaped legs. Before putting his car in reverse, he thought to himself that once again he was falling into a trap.

His action was what was expected of any character in a road movie: backing up to help them. Why was this story re-

peated time after time? The same old clichés, the same coincidences; this was the icing on the cake.

The older woman pulled her head out from under the hood and went to try to restart the engine. The younger woman turned to her and waved her hand. Her face reminded him of an old girlfriend. He stopped a few yards from her truck, got out and approached them, rolling up his shirt sleeves.

"Do you know something about motors, or are you just stopping to say hello?" the older woman growled sarcastically from the driver's window.

Peter looked at both of them, smiled and said, "Both."

The woman in the driver's seat suddenly pointed a two-barreled shotgun at him.

Pete reflexively raised his hands to protect himself. "Careful . . . careful . . . I mean no harm. . . . I don't even have a weapon."

"Are you sure?" the younger woman asked.

Peter lifted his shirt and slowly turned in a circle. "Clean."

"Lift you pants legs," the woman with the gun ordered. "Let's see your socks."

Peter did as she said and lifted his pants legs almost to his knees.

"Okay, okay. . . . What's your name?" the younger one asked more amiably as she approached him.

"My name is Peter and I'm on my way to Oro Valley to see some relatives."

The redhead smiled. "She's Laurie and I'm Valeria. As you can see, we transport horses. We're on our way to pick up a couple to take to Phoenix in under two days."

Peter went ahead and climbed onto the bumper by the truck's grill and stuck half his body in under the hood. "Let's see . . . if it's something simple, I can handle it. . . ."

Laurie and Valeria looked at each other.

"Do you have a flashlight, by any chance?" Peter asked.

"Here, take my keys . . . there's a little light on the chain, just press the button," Valeria said.

Peter took the keychain. It was a little while before he located the problem, fiddled around some and finally lifted his head above the engine. "I tightened the air filter that was about to fall off. You've got a shredded belt here that made the engine overheat. It's important for the engine's cooling system."

"For real?"

"In this desert heat, this must happen a lot," Peter said as he jumped off the bumper.

"Yeah, but when a guy is flirting, he'll saying anything to make an impression."

Peter cocked his head and said, "I always carry an extra belt, just in case . . . but it's for a car not a truck like yours."

The women exchanged looks.

"And what if we drive on until we hit a town?" Valeria offered.

"Driving slowly," Laurie added.

Peter stared at them for a moment and said, "I don't recommend it. You can completely burn out the thermostat, and that'll cost you a pretty penny. I really think you need to buy a belt and have it installed before going on. It's a simple job."

The women were silent. An eagle called in the skies above.

"Now what?" Valeria asked her partner.

Laurie raised her shoulders and said, "What do you think?"

Valeria passed the question to Peter.

Peter looked straight in the eye of the pretty redhead with the great body that for sure attracted him and sputtered, "I don't know . . . uh, buy one in the next town, I guess. . . ."

"That's it?"

"Yep."

"But where?" the older woman asked.

"No idea . . ." Peter said. "I'm not from around here either." He tried reading the sticker on the trucks windshield but couldn't make it out."

"Shit! We need to pick up those two horses within a couple of hours," Valeria said. "And the road signs are terrible," she complained.

Peter lifted his hand and showed them a piece of rubber. "I don't see how you're gonna get anywhere."

Valeria rubbed her chin in worry, and Laurie kicked at the gravel on the road's shoulder.

"If you want, I can take you to the next town to look for a belt . . . if there's one to be had," Peter ventured, looking down the lonely highway stretching from one horizon to the other.

"What about our truck?" Laurie asked, feeling responsible for the vehicle.

"Lock it up. What else?" Peter said. "Hopefully, there's something close by . . . but it looks pretty empty out here. . . . I mean, I don't think anyone's gonna steal it."

"Good thing we had no animals onboard. That woulda been a worse problem," Laurie said as she stepped down from the truck, the shotgun hidden under the driver's seat.

Laurie and Valeria exchanged looks, followed by Valeria and Peter.

4

The trio got into the car, with Laurie in the back seat and Valeria riding shotgun. For the next fifty miles Peter and Valeria found tons to talk and laugh about. Laurie's head fell to her chest, drifting off to sleep now and then. Valeria and Peter were in their element, narrating their life stories. They talked about music, commented on the landscape and a thousand other topics. After a while they found themselves in a town that two days later they'd leave to go their separate ways. As they drove in, the streets seemed abandoned, maybe because of the heat of the day and receding shadows as the sunlight grew more intense. They looked for an auto parts store—there was none. Finally, they found a mechanic, a man who was friendly enough. But he didn't carry the belt type they needed, he said, that they'd have to get one in the city that was a four-hour ride each way.

Valeria was crestfallen, Laurie cursed.

The mechanic said he'd fetch it because he had to pick up other parts there anyway, although he'd have to charge them extra for the service. The other option was to call the parts distributor directly and order the belt. But that could take up to two weeks. As far as the truck at the side of the highway, he'd go and tow it safely to his shop.

Laurie and Valeria agreed. In the scheme of things, it was no tragedy. They were grateful that it had happened before they were hauling the horses.

The trio ended up at a bar and ordered dishes of meat and potatoes, and beers.

Valeria excused herself, left the bar and found a pay phone in front of a hat store. She dialed a number automatically. In a matter-of-fact manner she told her boss what had happened, and the female boss could not hide her displeasure nor resist scolding Valeria. In the end, she said she understood and okayed paying for the repairs and the tow, but not the hotel room. The women would have to absorb that as a punishment. It was their fault the business was going to lose a profitable contract. Valeria had to plead forgiveness, although she did not know for what. "Accidents can happen to anyone," she wanted to counter, but decided to keep quiet. "How the fuck was I supposed to know a belt would break?" she wanted to scream at her boss, but she bit her tongue.

Peter and Laurie talked a while about car engines, food and beer while waiting for Valeria. He learned from masculine Laurie that she and Valeria were not mother and daughter, they were not even related. They worked for Louise, who was a veterinarian and owner of a ranch specializing in racehorses.

When Valeria returned, all three went to a motel and checked into separate rooms . . . although Peter and Valeria slept together. Two beautiful young bodies, shining on the bed, to the dampened sound of the TV, only witnessed by the revolving blades of the ceiling fan.

5

A few tanks of gas later and a stomach full of beer, Peter finally found himself in the town where he supposed both his uncles lived. It was a sad, arid place with the high-sounding name of "Oro Valley," that had obviously suffered the downside of globalization. It had lost population, mostly young people. Old folks were everywhere. It was a place lost in time, like an old, yellowed polaroid photo that refused erasure. He found the address he'd written down on a blue slip and went up and rang the doorbell. A young Asian-looking man opened the door and invited him in once he recognized his García surname.

In the living room Peter found a demented-looking man propped in a wheelchair absentmindedly watching television. Peter tried to address him, but the man did not even acknowledge his presence. No matter, Peter looked him over and informed him of his brother's death.

The young Asian man told Peter that his other uncle had died and that this one suffered from Alzheimer's. The old man suddenly looked at his caretaker with loathing and, after some gibberish, said he did not remember a thing. On hearing that his brother had died, he raised his shoulders and denied that he ever had a brother. Peter was disillusioned.

The young man walked to one of the walls and took down a picture, removed it from its frame and handed it to Peter. It was a photo of three happy young men sitting on a bridge. Peter recognized his father, whom he favored in appearance. In the photo his dad gestured playfully while embracing his brothers. Peter folded the photo, put it into his shirt pocket and thanked the young man, who showed Peter to the door. They said goodbye, addressing each other as "cousin."

Back in the sports car, Peter waited a bit before turning on the ignition. He looked at the photo again, this time more closely at uncles Rufino and Marcial with his father. He saw a family resemblance, but it was Rufino who looked the most like his father—he was the one who had fought in the Korean War and won a purple heart. Yes, Peter himself looked like Rufino. He smiled. "You can deny everything but your heritage."

Back on the road he thought of Valeria and came to the conclusion that his long journey had not been wasted, he had certainly not lost time. In the positive balance of things was that photo of his uncles when they were young in Texas. He had two loving memories to take with him. He smiled again. As for Valeria, he hoped to run into her again in this trip down memory lane, in the middle of the desert, in the road movie of his life.

"Valeria," he said out loud. He hoped to find her again, to make it all worthwhile again.

"Valeria!" he shouted out the window, and the echo repeated it twice, four times.

Valeria, who was asleep many miles away, heard him and smirked happily.

Peter pressed the gas pedal all the way to the floor.

The sports car is now just a red dot traveling across a canvas of an abstract painting of sand and yellow pebbles at dusk, accompanied by electric guitar music. The finishing touches are being applied by a conductor traveling in the past . . . although he too is not completely from there.

Happy endings are rare in road movies, especially when the protagonist is escaping and his life's love is passing by, or vice versa.

Loaded Dice

for Don Pilo

1

Karlos held a couple of wild cards in his hand, felt the win coming on, saw it clearly. How did he know he'd win? He had no idea, but whatever it was, he felt happy and self-assured. After gambling for so many years, he was experienced enough. The player across the table had nothing; Karlos had been counting his cards and surmised as much. The guy was one of those Gringo show-offs. Karlos raised the bet, and the other players threw in their cards. It was just the Gringo and Karlos now. "K," as he was known at the gambling joints, said to himself, *What did you think, Gringo? Did you think I had beginner's luck? Or that because I'm a Latino I'm an idiot?* K raised the bet again. It was obvious the Gringo was itching to rake in the pile of chips in front of him.

K for killer, for krafty, for kind.

The Gringo now made a show of tossing a roll of bills onto the pile of chips, thinking he'd force K to fold.

K paid up, using all but one of his chips. *If I lose, at least I'll have $20, just enough for a cab.* He smiled at his own sarcasm. K drew another card, worthless, placed it above his others, then lowered it on the table face down. The Gringo also drew a worthless card, but lowered it to the table in a nervous movement. They looked at each other, shooting darts. The atmosphere filled with hate.

It had been quite some time since Karlos had lost a sense of fear, especially when gambling. K looked at his challenger, feeling superior and amused; it was the stare of a wolf—his grandmother would have called it a foxy look. The Gringo revealed his hand and slapped it down on the table boorishly. A pair of fives. The onlookers gasped; those who had side bets raised their antes. The Gringo exploded with curses.

This was nothing more than another game, dammit, K told himself. Everything else, the provocations, didn't matter. He wouldn't be drawn into a fight. He repeated to himself, *As the saying goes, he who angers loses.* That asshole could call him whatever he liked; K had won and was ready to leave. He'd keep his cool, maintaining a calculated, strategic distance. These were the teachings of Chan Ho, his Taekwondo *sabom*, to whom he owed so much. *One always owes more to someone.*

Before showing his cards, K picked up his drink and drained it dramatically, before knocking on the table and showing his cards to the clown. He rearranged the cards in his hand and then laced them lovingly on the table, careful to follow gaming protocol. A royal flush. Applause. The onlookers celebrated, the betters clicked glassed with joy. "What a fuckin' hand!" someone shouted.

The Gringo was livid.

K could not help but smile. Cash. Enough cash to buy a decent car, one to take him to LA, where something, he didn't know what, was calling him. All he knew was that he had to go there—even his grandmother suggested it in one of her visits to his nightly dreams to educate him on various subjects.

As he swept the chips toward himself, K could not resist smiling and asked, "What did you think, that you'd buy the hand? You always need to know when to fold."

"What are you afraid of, Mexican? Let's keep playing," the Gringo said, trying to provoke K.

"Nope, I'm through for tonight."

"C'mon, one more."

K started piling the chips in stacks and sticking them in his jacket pockets without taking his eyes off of his challenger nor smiling at the people around them who looked on, some with envy, others anger, others in admiration.

"You're a coward, you little Meskin, like all ah your kind are."

That was an old overused tactic of a losing gambler: insult him to pull him in. Even K had used that one on occasion. K put on his dark glasses and faced him. "I've already won, Gringo. What else is there? And for your information, I have to hit the road early in the morning for a long trip. If not, I swear I'd keep playing, so's I could take you down for more. Have a nice evening."

"Let's play one more hand," the annoyed man yelled.

K finished pocketing his chips, except for three that he gave the croupier as a tip. He stood up to go to the cashier and then leave. He took three steps, turned and said to the loser, who was foaming at the mouth, "You should call it a night, too, Gringo. Anger is bad for the liver . . . you're getting paler."

2

The Castle was a mid-sized casino run by Native Americans, who by their ostentatious attire indicated that they were the owners and managers of the place. Karlos found an open seat that seemed to await him at the craps table with four other players. He ended up losing about half his cash with three rolls of the dice and decided to take a break. He left the dice behind, walked around and had a couple of beers. He had time on his hands, his gaming plans ruined. He was on his way to Los Angeles, for reasons not clear to him. Something was calling him there, something important. He savored his beer as he sat down at a table that allowed him to view all the action: the gamblers, the croupiers, the employees. He enjoyed sizing up the figures of the women who passed by. *Taking a woman to bed, though, takes time, imagination, money of course, but also control,* he was thinking. *Looking at a likely dame and approaching her, like a bloodhound . . .* He smiled, and his eyes widened as a dark young woman approached. Karlos looked her over from head to toe.

She was about five-foot-eight and wore a black dress, black net stockings, boots to the knee. Good legs and thighs, nice waist. Her pull was magnetic.

She was there for some reason, alone, drinking a daquiri and fiddling with her cell phone. Karlos approached her and made some insignificant comment, something about how the dice seemed loaded, how well the drinks were mixed at the casino or how the one-armed bandits were rigged. Then he invited her to join him at a gaming table.

They talked for awhile, then Karlos got sincere: "I don't know, but I have this feeling that with you beside me at the table my luck will improve."

"I'll improve your luck? Ha!" Ellen—that was her name—scoffed.

"I can almost feel it. It's like . . . a hunch. Let's call it that."

The dark young woman looked him up and down and smiled. "And me . . . what do I get out of it?"

Karlos smiled. She was direct—he liked that.

"Okay. Look, I only have a hundred thirty dollars to my name. I'll buy us a couple of drinks, no strings, and we'll bet the rest. If I lose, we say our goodbyes, and it'll be like nothing happened. But if I win, I'll give you a hundred, just like that. Whaddaya say?"

Now Ellen seemed intrigued, her eyes shining brightly. "How about you just pay me a percentage?"

"Of my winnings?"

"Of course," Ellen snapped back.

"How much?"

"You give me fifty percent."

"Ha-ha-ha, no way!" Karlos snapped back with a sly smile on his face. "I'll give you *fifteen*."

She thought it over for a few seconds and countered, "Thirty."

"I'll give you twenty-five, that or nothing."

Ellen laughed out loud and stuck out her hand. "It's a deal."

"Okay then, but you pay for the first round of drinks."

"The audacity!" she exclaimed, following Karlos in the direction of the craps table.

"Hey, hold on, wait!" she called.

Karlos backed up a few feet and took her by the arm. Full of confidence now, he whispered, "Now, we're gonna win, I'm sure of it."

Ellen just smiled.

And just like a couple who'd known each other for years, they crossed through the noisy section of slot machines, then the roulette and card tables with people milling all around them.

Karlos strode with pride. The beautiful woman on his arm was his lucky charm, just what he needed for a win that night. That's why he had come to the casino, to win, and he was not about to leave with empty pockets. That's also why he was headed for LA: to win. He knew it.

"How are you so sure that you're gonna leave here rich, K?" she asked. "Well, at least your name's easy to pronounce."

"Maybe not rich . . . but I'll leave with enough."

"Don't worry about it, I'll pay for the drinks . . . I was just joking," he said with an impish grin. "The day I can't pay for a lady's drink is the day I should call it quits."

Ellen laughed and gave him a childish look. This K inspired some weird confidence, as if they had known each other for years.

At the table, K asked for the dice, Ellen standing next to him. The croupier passed the dice to him in a leather cup. K shook the dice and then dropped them into the palm of his hand, feeling the dimension of the cubes, caressing them, weighing them. Ellen held his arm tightly, raised her shoulders and giggled. K asked her to blow on the cubes for luck. She blew seductively. Suddenly, K felt the blood course threw his veins at a hundred miles per hour, he was possessed, and he forcefully but gracefully launched the dice over the extent of the table. He envisioned the beauty on his arm in bed with him. The dice had shot out of his hand like bullets escaping a gun's muzzle, they crashed into the board at the end of the craps table, froze in the air for an infinitesimal instant and rolled on the green felt of the table. Ellen jumped with joy seeing that K had rolled a 4 to 1 pay-off. K had a broad smile on his face as he doubled his bet. It was his night. He ordered a couple of drinks, he felt renewed, pulled Ellen close to him and kissed her passionately. Suddenly, he felt a shiver, and instead of pleasure he felt something indescribable. He doubled his bet, picked up the dice and shook them. *What time was it when I came into this godforsaken casino?* He asked himself as the dice flew through the air like two magic stones with the woman's breath still caressing them.

Detour

---

for Jack Kerouac

Frank braked hard. He took the time to look for something good on the radio. A lively jazz number seemed better than that *cumbia* that had been playing. The car in front of him started rolling slowly, but only for a few yards before stopping again behind another one, which was behind another one and so on among the four lanes of traffic on each side of the highway. The jazz number ended, and he turned the radio dial again . . . he hated the damn commercials. He found a Bob Dylan song on an oldies station. Every day, same traffic, same time. He stepped on the gas just to lurch to a stop again. He placed the car in park and looked to his sides to see two other drivers like him, desperate, like dogs looking to protect their bones.

Frank ran his fingers through his hair. He would be late to dinner with Marianne. He could kick himself for not hitting the road before rush hour. Bob Dylan seemed too ludicrous at that moment with that song for college kids, and he decided to look for another station. A tango replaced Dylan in the car speakers. *Where the heck do all these jerks come from? So many cars!* He was more impatient than ever. He felt like a cigarette, despite having broken the habit a couple of months earlier.

He opened the glove box hoping to find a pack, but there was nothing. He slammed the glove compartment door shut. He braked again, the taillights of the car in front momentarily blinding him. He usually did leave the office before 5:45, sometimes he'd rush out even earlier. It was incredible, what a difference fifteen minutes made. What a time to receive a damn call, but what could he have done? Clients are and always will be clients. *Money, fuck it, it's what makes the world go round.*

The car crept up a few more yards. An anxious driver tried to get into the center lane, causing momentary chaos until the lines of traffic were re-established.

Again he changed radio stations. Again he put it in gear and then braked, placing his foot on the clutch and then the gas mechanically. He grabbed his head with his two hands and placed his elbows on the steering wheel. He was so late for dinner with Marianne. He needed to call her, cancel, but he knew what that would mean. As it stood, he was already on the outs with her. He had been late for the last two dates and now, a third one was about to crash because of the client's call. "You need to attend to women or they'll dump you for another guy, just like that," he remembered John saying, an office mate who practiced Spanish with him.

The car behind him honked, urging him to move forward. He looked into his rearview mirror: it was an old timer strapped to his seat as if it was the electric chair. It had been a rough day at work, full of stress and hurried decisions. It was date time. He looked at his watch. He pictured Marianne sitting in the restaurant with a cup of coffee while she waited for him. He wasn't going to make it. The line of traffic seemed infinite. On the radio he found a number by the Violent Femmes. He put the stick in neutral and lifted his foot off the clutch. What a goddamn parking lot the highway had turned into. A rescue helicopter was flying overhead, and in the distance he could hear sirens. *Just what I needed: an accident.*

Then, he remembered a shortcut that John had showed him the night they had decided to smoke a joint someone had given them during a demonstration in favor of legalizing weed. It was when they were stalled in the march and a beautiful black woman offered the joint to them like candy to a child. He looked at an upcoming sign. Maybe if he got off at the access road, he could get around the traffic snag. He was sure that the shortcut was nearby. He rolled forward a few more yards and saw that Exit 24 was two miles away. A good, round number; he was almost sure that had been the exit that he and his friend had taken that night—a good night it was, the same night he had met Marianne. He put on his blinker and crossed into the right lane suddenly, causing other drivers to honk. He got off the interstate and headed for a two-lane road and immediately felt relief. Another jazz number played on the radio. He began to relax. He'd call Marianne to plead forgiveness, she'd understand . . . at least he hoped so.

He searched for one of his cell phones in vain. *Shit! I left them in my suit jacket on the hook behind my office door!* He slapped himself on the forehead. *What an asshole!*

Frank rode the surface streets looking for a public phone, but, as in so many places, they had disappeared. *What can I do?* He decided it was better to hurry up rather than keep wasting time. He proceeded, crossed a bridge and drove up a narrow road that took him through a refinery. Very few cars under the starry skies. Then he started around some curves, noticing how the moon gave the trees silvery outlines. He stopped at a crossroads. At one side there was a small train stop and a gas station that looked closed. He got out of the car and went up to the windows of the gas station. He knocked on the door. It seemed abandoned, and he looked around trying to find some indication of where he was. He faintly remembered crossing through a forest with John, although he didn't remember a crossroads, nor the train stop. He was really lost. Forgetting his phone was the worst thing he could have done. He got back into the car and tried to find a station on the radio, but there was only static. *Strange,* he thought. *How far could he be from the city? Have I really gone that far afield?*

He finally found a Spanish-language station but could not understand a word. He stopped the car at another intersection, then turned right onto a large road, but one that was in bad shape with weeds overgrown on the shoulders and parts covered in water. He turned the FM dial back and forth again; the AM band was completely dead. He thought about Marianne. He pictured her at the cash register paying for her coffee, furious. He turned on his high beams. He suddenly braked when he noticed the road seemed to end abruptly. *Shit! What the hell is going on?* He crept forward. *What kind of road is this?* He regretted ever having left the highway. In third gear, he continued forward with the high beams on. Now the trees were just dark masses and the countryside was black. *Why aren't there any cars out here? Did I drive into private property? A road under construction? Part of the refinery?* He thought about retracing his way, but then nixed that. From the last crossroads to there had taken more than forty minutes, and he had already used up half a tank of gas. Going back was risky.

Just then Frank asked himself something that shook him to the root: *How did the Texas desert suddenly become a forest with giant trees?*

Afloat and Immobile

for Toño Alpízar

_I have been afloat in a swimming pool for more than half
my lifetime. Just barely staying
afloat. I pray to God not to make waves or noise that could
wake up the dwarf Poseidon who lurks under the calm waters
of this not-so-large pool, but big enough for me to drown in._

These images passed through my brain as I dozed in my
seat on the subway heading for Brooklyn. It had been an
exhausting day. I really felt beat after three shifts—I don't recommend that to anyone. But, hey, what can you do? Everything's expensive up here.

As soon as I sat down, my eyes began to close like shutters.
Just that fast. I don't usually sleep on the subway, you gotta be
careful, you know? We're talking about a dangerous underground train, pretty empty at two in the morning, although
there are always strange or curious-looking passengers you
need the be wary of. You know, drunks, desperados,
weirdos—some crazier than others—always looking for a fast
buck, ready to pounce on some fool or country bumpkin.

When I sat down, I fell into a really deep sleep. It didn't
help any that the night before my shifts I had stayed up watching an action flick, and I couldn't even remember what it was

about. I found myself floating, disoriented, inside the body of a stranger, not my own. Has that ever happened to you? And you ask yourself, "Who's that looking at me in the mirror?"

In my dream I dive into this large pool, under the cover of a large plastic tent held up by a rusty metal framework. Its four walls reaching up about thirty feet, it was a place once lighted in neon. There's only a small door at the far end of the pool from me. I can't hear anything, except for my breathing and splashing in the water. The water is shiny, black, thick and heavy.

I'm nobody to be interpreting dreams; I have no idea what they mean. I'm even worse at interpreting the visual images in dreams. I kind of remember that when I'm about to fall asleep and my muscles relax, I'm trying to reach the edge of the pool, but each stroke forward I swim seems to push me backwards, and from the bottom of the pool things float up: chairs, suitcases, a television set showing a war film, a table, kitchen utensils, a bed, small kitchen appliances . . . they're floating up like after a shipwreck. Water glasses, spoons, lamps. At first I was afraid, but I was soon terrified; the things floating so close to me made me nervous. I felt Death swimming towards me in those still waters.

Just then, the subway cop shook me awake. "We've arrived."

I was terrified. I had arrived at the end of the line and had to get out of the train.

I straightened up and got to my feet, rubbing my eyes. I begged his pardon and started walking slowly out of the subway car. It was not a pleasant dream, especially since it was silent, with no sound from the still waters, a black mirror reflecting me drowning. Just to remember that dream gave me goose bumps. I concluded two things: it was a troubling dream and it had really upset me . . . and also I was bothered because I was incapable of interpreting it. *What did that damn pool mean? And what about the objects that were floating near me?* I looked at my wristwatch, it was almost three in the morning. *Some night I've had!* I lifted my jacket collar and buttoned up and got ready to go out into the cold. Fortunately, I lived no more than twenty blocks from the station. I started walking.

Something else strange happened that night: it started snowing. It was the first time I had experienced snow. I'd seen it in films and had a vague idea of what it was. I felt the snowflakes on my face, my head as the landscape transformed quickly. I felt I had walked into another country where all those little white lumps danced in the air, covering everything and accumulating in piles. I picked up a bit of it and molded it in my hands. My face was numb, my nose freezing. I opened my mouth and stuck out my tongue to catch some of those flakes falling from the sky. They promptly melted. I'm sure I was smiling.

For someone like me who was born in the desert, to experience snow was one of those things I'll never forget. The snow covered the parked cars and the streets, and piles of it accumulated on the sidewalks.

As for the dream of the swimming pool, it returned a number of times, again in the subway during the next few months of that winter I spent in the city of cement and steel.

The Island within the Island

for my sister Sofia

"The sea is impressive, never looks the same, not even the same color. For three days now we've been pulled along by the wind continuing to fill our sails, making our masts and our bones creak. Our sails swell so much that those northerly winds lift us up high above the waves—we don't even touch them. Last night I was sure we were flying, so fast in fact that we had to grip onto the railing hard to keep from falling overboard. The wind finally ushered us to an island where, immediately, it died down to exactly where it is now. It just stopped and now . . . it stopped, it stopped . . . and that's how it's been every night."

The two young lovers exchanged quizzical looks while listening to the man speak.

"The island has fresh water and is surrounded by banks of many-colored fish. Since that night this has been my home. I've witnessed the most beautiful sunsets, night skies overflowing with stars, as well as every color imaginable in the sky. . . . It's incredible. At times when the wind returns in its full splendor, I can see up to a far distant point on the horizon, very far on the horizon that calmly looks back at me like the pair of very big blue but sad eyes of a woman. . . . You understand?" The old man ran through this litany to the young couple that had stopped to listen to him.

"It just may be the day speeding off in the distance, hoping to rest," the old man said, then looked at them in silence through glassy eyes and extended his sailor cap for a tip.

Once again the young lovers exchanged glances. The young man pulled some change out of his pocket and handed it to the old hippie-looking old dude. The girl smiled, not accustomed to such characters. In fact, she was totally amazed by New York City.

The dude put his old cap back on, kissed the amulet of love and peace he wore on a chain around his neck, and hobbled away among the trees, humming a century-old song, all performed in front of the couple that soon held hands and began walking again.

"Who is that guy?" the young woman asked, totally intrigued.

"Hmm . . . I have no idea . . . he's one of the hundreds of looneys that inhabit Central Park. He thinks that this place is surrounded by water, at least that's what he said . . . that this is an island within an island."

The girl's eyes grew wide in wonder. "If true, if I understood him, he was referring to a memory, or a boat that left him behind."

"He also said that the world begins and ends here."

"Poor guy . . . although he doesn't act like a crazy man."

"A friend of mine told me that he hasn't left this park in something like ten years."

They hurried across Fifth Avenue.

"How strange . . . although he really did know how to tell a story," she said approvingly.

Her boyfriend looked at her and remembered why he loved her so much. "Nah . . . he's just a senile eighty-some-thing, no one of consequence."

They kissed and continued on their way to the museum without even noticing the fish jumping around the park benches, the shells being deposited by the waves, the sand throughout Central Park, the coral reefs raising up to the sky, basalt columns, the island in the middle of the vastness, the island suspended between two oceans.

Lost & Found

1

Ramírez woke as the bus driver touched his shoulder and shook him. He opened his eyes, startled.

"Last stop. Time to get off!"

"Hmm . . . already?"

"Time to get off, we're here."

He wiped his eyes and looked at the impatient driver. "For real? Wow, I'm sorry, I guess I was really tired."

"I believe ya . . . you've slept for at least three hours since we arrived."

"No kiddin'?"

"Yep, and now I'm driving back."

"I'm very sorry," he said as he sleepily ran his fingers through his hair. He got up and followed the driver down the aisle of the empty bus.

The bus driver got into his seat and pressed the gas pedal down.

Disoriented, Ramírez said, "Excuse me, do you know if my suitcase stayed in the luggage compartment below?"

"All of the luggage was taken down. You need to go in and ask."

"Where?"

"I don't know ... I'm late," he grumbled as he adjusted the rearview mirror and pressed the gas pedal down again.

"Okay," Ramírez said and descended the bus steps to the ground.

The vehicle's door shut behind him and the bus took off with a blast of exhaust smoke. Ramírez found himself in a large parking lot. *But where? What city?* He looked around and saw four buildings with signs; A, B, C and D. He paused to think for a moment and then headed for the glass-covered building A. *That's probably where the luggage department is located.* He stopped at the entrance where people where milling around a long counter. On the wall he noticed a large clock but did not look at the time. He took another couple of steps, distracted by some kids playing with paper airplanes. He worked his way through the crowd to the counter for the Peter Pan bus line, even though he didn't remember the line he had traveled on. Along the counter there were signs for Greyhound, Wolf, Southwest Lines and Express Services. But he just could not remember which. He decided to head for the sign that read Lost & Found in green. The loudspeakers continuously projected women's voices announcing bus arrivals and departures. "Miss Libby Arnold, please go to window 22." He walked by a number of seated men and women awaiting their buses. Some were drowsing, others were benumbed, watching a large TV screen on the wall, and still others pretended to read their newspapers. He realized suddenly that he was thirsty and headed for the soda machine. He was momentarily reflected in the mirror on the instant photo machine, whose interior was flashing on and off. The curtain opened and a happy young couple emerged and embraced. The guy picked up the strip of photos, and they both smiled at the images.

Ramírez got to the soda machine, slipped five quarters into the slot and pressed the Coke button. He heard its rumble, opened the little plastic cover below and retrieved his can of pop. He opened it and took a large gulp, letting it fizz in his mouth and throat. He finished the soda in three gulps, throwing the can into the trash on his way to the Lost & Found window. He pressed a buzzer and saw a little man at the rear look up at him. The place was crowded with all kinds of boxes, suitcases, backpacks and packages with tags.

The man got up tiredly, came to the window and muttered, "How can I help you?"

"Good afternoon."

"Yes?"

"I lost my bag . . . well, actually, I didn't lose it, someone took if off the bus . . . I wasn't aware . . ."

The little man looked at Ramírez as if he had a screw loose. "If it's not lost, then why come here?"

"Uh . . . because I can't find it and I suppose it got misplaced."

"Hmm, I see. . . . What does it look like?"

"Oh, nothing special, you know . . . a black suitcase with squares on it."

The man looked into Ramírez's eyes and shook his head. "Do you know how many bags fit that description?"

Ramírez frowned and started to shake his head.

"Canvas or leather?" the man asked as he began writing in a notebook.

"Leather . . . more or less this size," Ramírez said, tracing the size in the air with his hands.

"On what bus line did you come?" he asked impatiently.

Ramírez raised his hands to the sides of his head. He just could not remember. *Why can't I remember? This guy is gonna think I'm looney, that I'm just wasting his time.* He decided to say the first name that came to him: "Greyhound."

"Okay," the clerk grunted, obviously in a bad mood. "That's something, at least." He proceeded to turn to a page in the middle of his notebook and ran his finger down a column of seemingly familiar numbers.

"You said, 'leather,' right?"

"Yes," Ramírez said as he looked to the rear, hoping to catch sight of his bag.

The little man perused more than four pages without success. "Under what name did you say it was registered?"

"I didn't say."

The little man flashed him a killer look.

"I didn't say, but my last name is Ramírez."

The clerk returned to his notebook, this time scanning the columns backwards.

"When did you say it got lost?"

"This morning."

"It's not here."

"The bus driver said they took it off the bus."

The little man suddenly banged the notebook shut and said, "Hmmm, I'm sorry, it's still too early . . . maybe we should wait awhile for it to show up."

Ramírez looked at him in distrust. *That's probably what he says to everyone who comes to bother him, a set phrase to get rid of them.* "Really? Maybe I can give you so more details. The blue squares on the bag have some bright red in them and the bag has a small yellow lock on the zipper. I'm worried, 'cause it's an expensive bag," he whispered as he handed the man a ten-dollar bill to soften him up.

The little man took the cash and opened the notebook up again. "Very well, Mister Ramírez, let's see . . ." This time he took about ten minutes to slide his finger down the columns of numbers in the worn-out notebook and finally concluded, "It's not here, Mister Ramírez, I swear."

Ramírez was deflated.

"Maybe it'll be here tomorrow."

"Whaddaya mean 'tomorrow,' I've got to leave, to continue on my trip," Ramírez pleaded.

"Ah . . . ," the little man uttered and started rifling the pages of his notebook again.

Ramírez looked around. "Maybe it's behind those boxes over there."

"Oh no, no way. It takes a while for the bags to get here."

"How come?"

"Yeah, that's what I ask myself. Are you sure it was a Greyhound bus?"

"Uh . . . ye . . . ," he began to stutter.

"What can I do? Your bag just isn't here. Look for yourself," the little man said as he pushed the notebook to Ramírez.

Ramírez drew close and tried to read the columns of numbers and letters that meant nothing to him. "I don't understand any of it."

"Me neither."

"I mean the numbers, and those columns and stamps . . ."

"Of course, not. . . . It's written in code. If it weren't, how do ya think we'd find anything? For instance, here: the two last digits are the bus driver number . . . the 2 and the 8 are the bus line and the other three numbers mean the date and time when the object was reported lost. As you can see, everything's very clear. When it's under someone's name, their name is the first thing noted, like it is here."

"Yes, I can see it now."

"Let me see your bus ticket," the clerk suggested.

Ramírez searched the pockets of his pants, jacket and shirt. Empty: no money except for a few quarters, no credit cards, not even his driver's license. He felt ridiculous. *That damned bus driver must have cleaned me out before waking me up.* He held back curses so as not to insult the little man who already thought he was crazy. "I think I left it on the seat in the bus . . . ."

The little man shot him a look of disgust. "That is just unbelievable! How dare you waste my time! You don't have anything to prove your identity?! Are you just trying to steal a bag or something? Who do you think you are? Do you think that for a stinking ten bucks I'm just gonna hand you a bag that doesn't belong to you? 'Cause you sweet talk me? How dare you complain!"

"I'm sorry, man . . . I'm very sorry. You know . . . I fell asleep and I guess that one of the passengers"—he resisted accusing the bus driver—"took my wallet and money . . . well, the rest of my money," he said, his voice trailing off.

"You expect me to believe that? You could be lying again."

"I'm not lying, I swear."

The phone rang and the little man ambled over to his desk and picked up the receiver.

Ramírez once again looked around at all the bags piled on the shelves against the wall and everywhere. He needed to find his bag more than ever because he remembered hiding three thousand dollars in rolled up hundred dollar bills among his socks and shirts. *How in the world did I fall asleep? Damn. How did I not notice what bus line or the number on the bus driver's badge? What an idiot I am.* He banged the bars on the Lost & Found window and suddenly remembered an argument he and his wife had, although he didn't remember what they argued about. He remembered her gesticulating and then picking up a knife. Just then, he understood why he was traveling, why he was here. He wanted to travel incognito.

The little man hung up the phone and returned to the window. "Well, my friend, are we done?"

With a worried grimace, Ramírez said, "Would you do me a big favor? Could you let me in and look for it real quick . . .

then I'll get out of your hair, whether I find it or not. I swear, really quick."

"You've got a lot of nerve. How dare you even think I would do that. You must think I'm stupid. Who says you're not a thief or a criminal? Here behind the glass and bars I'm safe, and that's why you're being friendly. But what if you have a knife hidden in your jacket, what if you stab me in the ribs . . . ?"

"Look, mister, I pay taxes, I have a paying job and two daughters I'm dying to see. All I did was fall asleep on the bus and lost my ticket stub. Yes, I am bothering you, but none of this is criminal behavior. I just need this little favor . . . from one human being to another. That suitcase had all my belongings, including—"

"No, sir," the clerk interrupted. "Maybe you think I'm dumb or something."

"Please, mister, if you want, I'll take my jacket off. . . . Look, you can see for yourself: nothing. Okay? I'm a decent person, I'm a doctor. Do me this little favor, please. I'll look for the bag and then I'm gone."

The little man looked him over from head to toe. "Are you really a doctor?"

"Yes, honest."

For a minute the little man seemed to acquiesce, at least calm down some. "Okay, let me ask my supervisor."

Ramírez smiled slightly, thinking he had won the man over.

"So, you'll let me in?"

"Tomorrow."

"Tomorrow? Why?"

"My supervisor has already gone home. Almost everyone's left. Do you know what time it is?"

Ramírez looked down at his wrist where he used to wear his watch.

The clerk beat him to it and said, "It's almost six. You'll have to wait."

Ramírez looked up at the giant clock on the wall. It really was six o'clock.

The little man looked at his own watch and added, "It's almost time for me to leave, too."

"What time does your boss come in in the morning? Isn't there a second shift tonight?"

"Just tomorrow, as I've said three times already . . . after 9:30 am."

"Okay, so . . . maybe I'll find it behind that pile over there," he said, pointing.

"No, that pile and the one behind it are yesterday's bags."

"Hey, I'll be quick." Ramírez was desperate. He couldn't explain it, his stomach was unsettled, like he was nervous and had left something unfinished.

"Who do you think you are? That could cost me my job. I, too, have children and a wife I need to support."

"Put yourself in *my* place."

"You put *your*self in my place."

Ramírez looked at him in disgust. All of this was absurd, absurd, absurd. A woman's face came to him, although in his mind he couldn't make out her features . . . a young smiling woman, pretty, who was opening her arms to him."

"Tomorrow then."

Ramírez resigned himself, shrugged and said, "What else is there?"

The telephone rang again.

"Okay, until tomorrow. I have to finish up a few things before I leave," the clerk said and shut the window.

Ramírez walked up to a column, leaned against it and looked around. It was a bus station like any other: ticket windows, rows of seats, a fast-food court, stores and newsstands. People everywhere, some getting in lines to board buses, people waiting and watching TV, others dozing off. It was a place of transit. He started to walk toward a seat in front of the TV, but he hated football and preferred the news or a movie or any other sport. He sat down instead in a seat with its own television set attached. He slid two of his last three quarters into the slot and picked out an old Judy Garland film that he didn't make it through. He yawned, about to take out his last quarter, but thought better of it. He'd save the coin for a possible phone call later. He closed his eyes in boredom, even though he was still anxious and despite the hard seat, the loud PA system and the cold air rushing in through the bus gates. Time had never passed so slowly for him. There was nothing to occupy his mind until around 5 am, when a teenage girl who had been tossing and turning in a sleeping bag on the floor came up and sat down next to him. Ramírez felt her presence and opened his eyes.

She took a sip from a large bottle of water and said, "Hi."

Ramírez straightened up and acknowledged her. "Hi."

"Were you able to sleep a little?" she asked and took another sip of water.

"Not really," Ramírez confessed and placed a hand to his backside. "You know, these seats are horrible."

"You got that right. I even think they make them that way on purpose . . . you know, so people won't be able to sleep while they wait for their buses."

"It's not fair. Did you sleep any?"

"Yeah, I slept a bit. But anyway, the floor is much better than these seats, you know?"

"Why?"

"Well, you know, I'm a female . . . and the seats are more dangerous if you let your guard down."

"Oh, yeah?"

"Anyway, I'm used to my sleeping bag."

"I see."

"Madelyn," she said, extending her hand.

"Ramírez."

"Where are you headed?" she asked as she zipped up her jacket.

"I live in Orlando . . . I mean, I'm going to Orlando," he said, reminding himself that he was traveling incognito.

"Nice. . . . It's pretty there, right?"

"Uh, more or less. The climate's great."

"I have a friend who went to Orlando. His parents took him to an amusement park there."

"Yes, there are a bunch, but they bore me, I don't know . . . and where are you headed?"

"I'm going to visit my parents . . . in Washington state," she said and took a large sip from her water bottle that seemed forever full.

"Where are you coming from?"

"Montgomery."

"What's in Montgomery?"

"Nothing special: poor people, rich people. Rabid cops, the Alabama River. . . ."

"Interesting."

"If you say so."

"What I say is, I hope we can get to our destinations on time."

"What time do the ticket windows open?" she asked as if trying to cut the personal questions.

Ramírez understood and said, "I'm not sure, but I hope it's soon . . . I've been told around 9 am."

Then she announced, forlorn, "I lost my suitcase. I thought I saw it on the luggage conveyer belt, but, *boom,* it disappeared."

Ramírez looked at her in shock. "Me too."

"It's horrible, it really bums me out. Grrr, I'd like to punch myself in the face."

"That's how I feel. I don't know how it could have happened, darn it," Ramírez said and gripped his head with his hands.

"I can't understand it, and here I am waiting for them to open that damn window, when I should be at home getting ready for the wedding."

"Who's getting married?"

"My older sister, tomorrow . . . it's gonna be a big shindig . . . and here I am, screwed!" She shot up and stamped her foot on the floor.

"I'm so sorry."

"Don't be. I've got a lot of defects."

Ramírez just listened.

"I'm always late, and then I'm always running to catch up."

"Me too," Ramírez commiserated, but tried to imagine the other defects of the redheaded teenager with the languid look that reminded him of his daughter.

The girl leaned over to him and whispered, "That guy, too." She pointed at a man in his forties who was leaning against a wall and trying to sleep.

"What?"

"He lost his bag, too."

"How do you know that?" Ramírez asked, looking the man over.

"He told me. We were talking early in the evening, around dinner time."

"Wow . . . what bad luck," Ramírez said. "That makes me feel a little better . . . you know, that I'm not the only one. There's three of us."

"Three? What about the rest of us? There's more."

"These bus lines are so damn incompetent."

Now it was she who gave him the once over. "Okay, I'm up and out, gotta pick up my sleeping bag. And I'm dying for a coffee."

Ramírez nodded and then began to think: the girl's features reminded him of someone. *Could all those people be waiting on their lost bags? No!* He began to sweat at the idea. He looked around, then turned around: the place was crowded. It was at least twice the number of people than when he had arrived, although he swore he saw people with suitcases, people getting on buses, getting off buses, leaving. He tried to erase that idea from his mind. *Can there be so many of us? And, what the hell am I doing in this damn station when I usually travel by air?* He crossed his arms. The arms on the clock seemed to not be moving at all. *I need to relax.* He closed his eyes and remembered that he hadn't asked the girl the name of her city. *Not important.* He relaxed his shoulders and yawned. He dozed a bit, and imagined two headlights coming at him, a crash through the door, screams, his hands bloodied. . . . He sprang up and instinctively looked at the clock: 7:30 am. *A couple more hours, a couple, and I'm out of here.* He returned to his hard, plastic seat and tried to calm down.

As never before, not since his school days, he wished that it was 8:30 in the morning. He stood up again and crossed the room to lean his tired humanity against a column. He was exhausted. Then he noticed that some people had coffee and donuts in their hands. The cleaning people were starting work, and the people sleeping on the floor had to get up. Coffee would be a good way to start his day, he'd get a decaf. But then he remembered that he only had a quarter to his name. Maybe he could buy candy or some French fries. He went up to a vending machine and inserted his quarter. It promptly delivered a milk chocolate bar with peanuts. It had been more than twenty years since he had eaten anything like that. He envisioned himself on duty at the hospital and the blurred face of the woman he had been trying to recall. He unwrapped the chocolate and went to sit down in a seat where someone had left the television on. He passed the time looking at an old war movie and devouring that heavenly bar of chocolate. Before he could enjoy the end of the movie, a sign flashed on the screen instructing the viewer to insert another coin. He swallowed the last of the chocolate, stood up and threw the wrapper in the garbage. He entertained himself looking at the Departures board: Cleveland, Denver, Minneapolis, Salt Lake City, Detroit, Atlanta, Houston, Dallas.

The hour hand on the clock arrived at 8 like bells ringing in his head. He breathed in deeply and headed for the Men's room. He needed to talk the Lost & Found attendant into letting him look for his luggage. He needed to get back on the road. The tip he gave the man should help, but if it became necessary, he would speak to his supervisor, or whomever, in order to find that bag that held all his belongings. What most worried him were those three thousand dollars and the credit cards he had hidden inside. Without them, he could not travel anywhere. He was sure that he could solve the problem quickly, because he needed to continue his journey. He washed his face and rinsed out his mouth, but sorely missed his toothbrush and his razor.

On exiting the restroom he encountered a long line of people, including the girl he had befriended, in front of the Lost & Found window. Seeing that line immediately put him in a bad mood. He hadn't waited all night to have to now get into a long line that seemed to be growing as he watched. He decided to go up front to talk to the little man, who'd surely recognize him. He unobtrusively sidled up to the window, taking care that the girl or the man behind her in line would not notice him. At the window, the little clerk was in a heated argument with a man who apparently did not have a receipt or remember on what bus he had traveled. The little man shook his head in a furor. Ramírez decided to wait a bit, seeing it was not a good time to speak with the clerk who had turned into a mad man.

Ramírez joined the crowd of onlookers as the little man slapped his notebook shut, sent the customer on his way and closed his window. It looked like that was his response to everyone. He turned and went to his desk, removed some papers, picked up the phone and dialed a number. The onlookers exchanged puzzled looks, not knowing what else to do. A young man not more than twenty years old was up on his tiptoes, pointing beyond the window; he began hollering that he recognized his bag in back. He was happy, fulfilled, as the little man approached with disgust on his face to re-open the window.

"Yes, what can I help you with?"

Ramírez pondered how much the little man loved that worn-out phrase. He was beginning to abhor that little rat in that cage behind the glass and bars.

"Back there on the pile of bags!" The young man could not restrain his glee. "My luggage!"

The little man reluctantly opened his notebook, impervious to the enthusiasm of the smiling young man.

Ramírez felt sorry for the stoop-shouldered, sickly-looking little mouse, who outside of his little cage was a nobody, a shadow being lost in the masses of people he despised. Ramírez stepped back a couple of steps, trying to avoid being spotted by him.

"My bag! That one over there, under the red one and the brown one in the second pile!" shouted the teenager as he gripped the bars on the window.

The little man searched through at least three pages of his notebook and finally opened his mouth: "Do you have a receipt?"

The young man pushed a lock of hair out of his eyes. "Yes, here it is," he proudly announced as he produced it from the inside pocket of his jacket without handing it over.

"Let me see it."

The young man watched warily and turned to survey the onlookers as if trying to secure witnesses and finally gave the receipt to the clerk, who took it and matched the number to a cypher in his notebook.

"Yep, that bag is yours. You've got great eyesight. Congratulations."

The young man was beaming.

"Just one thing, though . . ."

"Yeah?" said the young man, his face suddenly reflecting dread.

The witnesses watched with bated breath.

"It wasn't your turn. There are a whole bunch of people in line a head of you . . . who got here early."

The young man was dumbfounded, as if he could not believe his ears.

"Get in line, my friend, and I'll take care of you when it's your turn."

The people in line agreed. "Yes, in line," someone yelled.

The young man resigned himself and walked to the end, dragging his feet, and disappeared from Ramírez's line of vision. The first person in line started asking about some boxes he described. The little man attended to him in the habitual way: how could he help, his receipt, the description, blah, blah, blah.

Today, there was a machine dispensing numbered tickets, and a loudspeaker instructed everyone to take one to get to the window in order. The crowd dispersed, and things calmed down. Ramírez took a seat, this time in front of the screen listing arrivals and departures. He began to yawn. Now, the line seemed incredibly endless, and he started in on cursing his stupidity. He really needed some sleep, and his eyes began to close just as his stomach began tightening with anxiety. Once again, that blurry image appeared to him: a car twisting in the air and crumbling as it hit the pavement. Someone's bloodied face, words without meaning, a scream. He jumped up from his seat and opened his eyes wide. Nothing around him had changed; people in the same line paging through magazines, chatting, looking at the clock, the television, simply waiting their turns.

Ramírez stretched out his arms and yawned. The line kept getting longer. He noticed that the young man who had identified his bag was quickly getting closer to the window. He stopped for a second, said something to a man who cut in front of him and pushed him away.

"I demand my suitcase!" he yelled, completely beside himself.

The little clerk responded, "We have rules! Can't you see?"

"Like I give a fuck! I want my bag!"

"If you don't wait in line until it's your turn, you won't get it!"

The youngster grabbed the window bars and yelled, "You go to hell! I'm not gonna wait another day in those back-breaking seats!"

"Please, for the last time! Get out of here, sit down, take a number and get in line, and let me do my job!" the little man barked, staring daggers at him.

"If you don't give me my bag, motherfucker, I'll go in and get it myself!"

The little man stuck his head up to the window cage and said, "Oh yeah? I'd like to see ya try it! That door's designed to keep an elephant out."

"Really? And how about a Molotov cocktail, fucker?" he said smiling.

"You'll be sorry you said that, buster!" the little man warned, ran to the telephone and quickly dialed a number.

The young man ran toward the food court, then returned brandishing a metal bar and started beating on the Lost & Found door, all the while blasting out curses.

The little man, in the meantime, leaning on his desk, dialed again, this time to the police.

Madelyn, the girl from last night, and a young black man with an afro joined in trying to bust the door down, kicking it and beating it with a garbage can.

The line of people suddenly became a circle of bodies, incited by the violence and screaming for their bags, lost and misplaced possessions. But they soon dispersed as a squad of police, who without so much as a warning, started attacking people seated in the waiting area, including Ramírez. Now, the crowd grew and started shouting at the police. One man was bleeding profusely from a wound on his face. The police had obviously beat him with a club.

"Pigs! Why did you hit him?!"

"Damn you all! He was only sleeping there!"

The aggressive policemen smiled behind their transparent face shields as they slowly moved forward. A young man ran up and gave one of the cops a few karate kicks that took him down. Then he ran into the crowd for protection from two cops pursuing him. The crowd cheered, and the police froze in front of the threatening wall of fists and feet preparing to attack them. The cops swiped the air with their clubs and retreated two steps. This was followed by the crowd advancing two steps. Then a can of soda crashed into the helmet of one of the cops, who collapsed to the floor like a cloth doll. The cops retreated further as the euphoric crowd screamed for the heads of the policemen.

"C'mon, you cowardly pigs!"

The police were stunned.

The Karate Kid, Madelyn and The Afro—who turned out to be a neo-anarchist—stepped up and challenged the cops with obscene gestures.

Just then, a second squad of cops appeared at the main entrance, joined the others and marched forward brandishing their clubs.

2

The clash was inevitable, and soon the civilians and the police were battling each other to the sound of banging and beating, screams. There were wounded people lying on the ground bleeding, others were dashing away in fear. The scene transpired in slow motion before Ramírez's eyes from his vantage point along a wall. He had no idea what to do, he could not believe his eyes. He actually detested violence. Absorbed by the unfolding battle, out of the corner of his eye he saw a policeman about to strike him with a club. He ducked and moved a couple of feet. Because he had served in the Marines, he reflexively landed a kick to the cop's body, then another one, although the cop was able to slap the club across Ramírez's knuckles. Ramírez fell to the floor, writhing in pain.

A young man came up behind the cop and bashed him on the helmet, sending him to the floor. Ramírez thanked him and got up. Now, he wasn't just upset but truly offended. *Why did that damn cop attack me? Why are they beating on women and children?*

He turned and saw a large contingent of cops storming in through a side entrance, some of them on horses. A molotov cocktail exploded in front of the horses and they reared up and dumped their riders. A second molotov exploded among the cops on foot, who tried to escape in the direction of the food court. Groups of teenagers were ripping up those horrible plastic seats to assemble them into a barrier as a group of riot police took up position in the center of the station. They wore gas masks and carried machine guns and plexiglass shields. From behind the crowd of civilians, a can was launched and reached all the way over to split a horse's head open and cause the animal to fall to its knees. The crowd broke out in cheers, and the police responded by launching tear gas canisters left and right. The crowd retreated to the perimeter. Another group of young people lighted a bonfire to counter the effects of the gas while others kept bombing the police with cans that shot out colored soda in every direction. A number of cops were out cold on the floor. A wedge of police advanced from the left to mow down various civilians. A teenager covered in blood was dragged to safety by two women trying to tend to the wounded. An old lady, wearing broken eyeglasses, was sobbing as she crawled around looking for the shoes she had lost. The police continued to surge as the Karate Kid grappled with two cops. Madelyn and the young anarchist were tossing back tear gas canisters at the surging police as if they were in a tennis match. "Fuck you, pigs!" they kept shrieking.

Ramírez ran to help an old man who was being trampled under a horse. He grabbed him by the shoulders and dragged him to one of the columns. Then he ran to pick up a toddler who was bawling uncontrollably amid the frenzy and sat him down next to the old man. Ramírez wiped his brow only to realize that he was bleeding, so he took out his handkerchief and held it to his forehead. His shirt was bloodstained, his left hand was swollen and discolored and he was wired. He heard a wild scream and lifted his face to see four cops standing over the fallen anarchist, beating him mercilessly. Ramírez stepped behind the column and observed, not comprehending how he had ended up in this ridiculous field of battle. A gas canister rolled to his feet spewing out its poison in whitish gusts. He picked up the hot projectile and ran to the Lost & Found window and threw it in, to the surprise of the little man, who immediately began to choke and cough.

A few feet away, Madelyn was lying unconscious on the floor, seemingly asleep on her backpack, bleeding from her nose and mouth. Ramírez suddenly realized he hadn't brought along his medical bag. . . . *Where did I leave it?*

Now, the police were shooting rubber bullets that were bouncing around everywhere, leaving little black marks. A bullet hit Ramírez in his left shin, and he screamed in agony. Another hit him in the arm. He took cover behind the television monitors that were shooting out sparks. He looked up and saw a policeman fall from his horse enveloped in flames. He noticed a group of teenagers were able to escape out the side doors and felt happy for them. He dropped to his knees in order to hide from the police and their onslaught. He heard a ruckus behind him and saw the little man fleeing his bunker. His eyes popping, his mouth wide open gasping for air, the clerk fell to the ground convulsing. Stooping over, Ramírez ran to him, then over him and into the Lost & Found, all the while holding his nose. He began to search desperately for his bag, as if it was all that mattered in the world, while the battle ensued

outside. He heard sirens, loud crying, crackling radio commu-
nications, objects hitting walls, glass breaking.

His bag was not on the shelves. He opened closets and
dumped boxes and packages on the ground . . . no luck. He
needed that damn bag more than ever; it was all that he had
left after the divorce. *What horrible luck!* He had packed his
diary in the suitcase, and now he couldn't even remember his
brother's telephone number, not even his address. "Goddammit!" he howled in exasperation. He went to the clerk's
desk and discovered a door behind it, but it was locked. It
seemed important, and he searched the desk for keys. The
third drawer he opened had the keys, and he was able to open
the door. He went in and saw a spiral staircase descending
into the dark. He looked for a light switch—there was none.
He returned to the desk and found a flashlight and used it to
light his way down the spiral of black stone stairs. He stopped
suddenly, almost losing his balance where the stairs ended before reaching the ground. His heart was beating wildly. He
tried to focus in the dark. It smelled musty, humid. There was
luggage everywhere, bags upon bags upon bags. He couldn't
believe his eyes. It was incredible. He ran the flashlight's beam
over the enormous piles of suitcases and boxes. *Am I dreaming or have I gone mad?* It was incredible, but real. He calculated the distance between the last step he was on and the
ground, and decided to jump down.

3

He suddenly found himself standing on a giant mountain of
suitcases, valises, bags, trunks, backpacks, portfolios and things
lost over who knew how many years, maybe even decades. The
beam of light revealed no end to the cavernous cellar. He could
not believe his eyes. He just could not comprehend what he was

seeing; it was like nothing he'd ever witnessed. In the distance he saw numerous mountains of luggage of various colors and materials. He was baffled. He squatted and picked up a large, heavy briefcase with belts around it; he couldn't open it. He took a couple of steps, lost his footing and tumbled down the mountain, laughing like a child, although he should have feared for his life. He landed hard and sat down on a carrying case for a bass fiddle. He got up and walked gingerly among all sorts of bags: square, round, brilliantly colored ones and sober ones, some durable materials and metal, others made of plastic, canvas, leather—some with chrome borders, designs. . . . Some were made in the 1940s, others during the dark 50s, the fabulous 60s, the crazy 70s, the hilarious 80s and even the scary 90s. It was unbelievable: an exhaustive collection of luggage in disarray. Some had combination locks, others simple little locks on the zippers, others had nothing whatsoever. Others were open and empty of clothes as if their owners had forgotten to pack. He picked up a small, light blue bag with white edges and rested it on his knees. He gave it a turn and decided to open it, and an acrid smell issued from the antique bag. He could see in the light beam that the women's clothes inside were still folded perfectly. There was also a round mirror set in silver, a tortoise shell brush and a small case with feminine items: lipstick, earrings, nail polish, eyeliner, hand cream and a dried up tube of toothpaste.

Ramírez smiled at his inner voyeur. He placed everything back where it was, carefully closed the case and set it on a larger bag, which had a chain around it with four combination locks. *It must have contained something of great value to its owner.* He unzipped another suitcase that contained a collection of art pieces: a fuchsia-colored chess set, a Bible with gold edging and a small, beautiful dagger with precious stones in the handle, along with some neckties, socks and leggings.

Ramírez thought about keeping the dagger, but decided against it, thinking that for some reason it would be disloyal. He put everything back, closed the bag and leaned it against the other one. He stood up and moved down a few feet, where a trunk large enough to fit a man caught his attention. It was very heavy and locked. He looked it over closely: the humidity had decayed its leather, and it was covered with decals from the era of the Third Reich. He opened another bag and found a New York City souvenir art-deco magnifying glass, a pair of hand-stitched lady's two-tone shoes and a Great Gatsby-style comb. He picked up the shoes, which were tiny, and tried to envision their owner: bobbed hair, black silk stockings, light garter belts, a slim cigarette in her hand and a grey felt hat above a Greta Garbo smile. *Where was this woman heading when she lost her belongings? For an audition in Hollywood?* He picked up a red suitcase. *How does one decide what to pack for a trip? How does someone decide what to leave behind?* Inside, the bag was packed with cotton clothing, and in the side compartments there were some photos: rough-looking men in basic clothes, thick hands, heavy hats and coats for cold weather. He closed the bag and picked up another. *What am I doing?* he asked himself with a shudder. He got up without shutting the bag, and its contents fell out. He moved ahead without bothering to pick them up.

As he preceded, he came upon an antique-looking trunk with rusted hinges turned upside down. He pushed it over and was able to open it. Inside it were photos of heavy-set women wearing loose dresses; they had large breasts and sad but purposeful visages. In one compartment there were snapshots of men who looked like immigrants, perhaps Italian, Irish or Scottish, obviously poor, judging by their clothes; they had that languid look of having left something irreplaceable behind. He returned the photos to their place with care. He stood up and looked around, thinking that perhaps these were the bags of all the immigrants who had never made it to their destination. A chill ran up his spine.

He thought of his family, his daughters, and became very anxious. He was dying to see them, touch them, tell them how much he loved them. *What the heck am I doing in this godforsaken place? Am I dreaming? What a convoluted history these Greyhound employees have had! To hell with my bag. What do I care for any of my stuff, even the $3000? To hell with it all.*

He decided to backtrack and began climbing up the mountain of bags, but the ascent seemed endless. He took off his jacket, feeling overheated and thirsty. He trudged onward, he couldn't say for how long, until the batteries started giving out in his flashlight. When he arrived at the mountaintop and he could hardly see anything. He perceived shadows that seemed to move, heard whispers on a slight breeze coming in from somewhere. *Where am I, really?* He was exhausted and decided to sit down. His hands landed on an old brittle newspaper, which turned out to be *The New York Times* for November 11, 1918, Armistice Day. He started to read, but the batteries finally gave out. He closed his eyes, feeling very tired, and reclined into a deep sleep.

He is arguing with his wife as she gets into the car. She has found out about his lover and is berating him, knowing that the medical conference he went to in Ontario was a cover for his adultery. He's a liar, an unfaithful cur who runs away from his responsibilities, a heartless, uncaring father of his two daughters asleep in the back seat.

4

He woke up very early in the morning, although he couldn't say what time it was without his wristwatch. There was a bit of light, a faint blue light coming in from somewhere. He rubbed his eyes, made a 180-degree turn. All around him were bags, hundreds, thousands, maybe millions of them, spread out into an unknowable distance. He stood up. Again, he wished he were dreaming, but everything was too real, so much so that he was deathly afraid and wanted to go back, escape from where he had entered.

Suddenly, in the distance he saw a human figure sitting on top of a tall mountain of luggage. He took cover behind a large trunk which had been thrust open. He spied the figure through a hole next to the clasp. From his trench, he observed the figure for more than twenty minutes. The figure didn't seem crazy, despite being bare footed and unclothed. Ramírez emerged from his hiding place and raised his hand in an attempt to catch the attention of the person, who only looked off into the infinite distance. Ramírez raised both hands then, hollered and waved his arms, but the man did not acknowledge him.

He decided to go up to him. He descended his own mountain and climbed the other to within fifty yards of the man. Again, he waved his arms and hollered. The man stood up reluctantly. He seemed surprised, even baffled, by Ramírez's presence. Finally, he acknowledged Ramírez's greetings and waved his arms, smiling. Ramírez took this as a sign to approach. He had to get around a large wall of luggage and descend a small hill of bags. The man started walking toward him, seeming to know the terrain, where to step and where to jump without slipping. Ramírez, a novice in that terrain, started toward him, slow and careful so as not to trip.

Ramírez observed him like a boy envious of a more agile playmate. Every few steps they looked at each other so as not to go the wrong way. Ramírez should have been terrified but ignored his fear in hopes of finding a logical explanation—he was a medical doctor, after all, a man of science, a man obsessed with the truth. He wanted the man to explain where they were, what they were doing there and, basically, how to get out, which was his main concern. Ramírez rested a moment on an enormous bale of clothing; he was exhausted, sweating in the musty air.

After about an hour, they were finally able to sit down together and look each other over. The man wore a loose-fitting civil-war jacket and an infantry shirt from World War II. He sat on a Stradivarius violin case that belonged to the very violin the man held below his chin, attempting to play Paganini's *Capriccio*.

Ramírez smiled, realizing for the first time that all of this was comical. The man finished playing the composition, closed his eyes and raised the violin high. What else could Ramírez do but applaud?

The man extended a dirty, calloused hand and said, "Today, I am Mark."

"Ramírez."

They shook hands.

"How do you like the landscape?" Mark asked in a sarcastic tone that puzzled Ramírez.

"Honestly, I don't."

"That's too bad. You see that mountain?"

"Yeah, what about it?"

"I suggest you never go near it . . . good thing you didn't keep going that way." He looked deeply into Ramírez's eyes. "Let me explain. One time, many years ago, a tornado battered the city. It flooded everywhere, including the public library, city hall and, of course, here as well. You should have seen it. In some places the water rose more than ninety inches. The water got in through the cracks in window sills . . . ."

Ramírez looked around and wondered what windows he was talking about. *How long ago had that happened? Has this madman lived down here since then?*

"What I advise," the man said as he got to his feet, "is you not go in that direction. I think it's about twelve-feet deep and the bags floated over it. The last time someone came to visit me it was an employee—I can't remember from which bus line—and he was looking for his girlfriend's bags. He wouldn't listen to me, didn't believe me . . . what happened was that he tried to grab onto those decaying ones . . . and two hours later he sank. He thought I'd rescue him . . . impossible, I told him, just like I'm telling you now. I was very explicit."

This guy is *insane*, Ramírez thought as he stood up. He looked around, searching for the entrance, the spiral staircase he remembered. Nowhere to be seen. The place was unimaginably large, simply immense. The staircase seemed to have dissolved. The place seemed to be limitless, with no horizon in sight. *Where the hell am I?* He formed a mental picture of himself amid that endless span of trunks and suitcases. . . . He was a caricature, an absurd figure, an apparition.

"Anyway, I'll see you later," Mark said as he placed the violin in its case.

"Wait," Ramírez begged. "Where are you going?"

"That way," he said, pointing into the distance. "It's an area I'm not familiar with. I've been looking for a jewelry box inside a suitcase, and in the box is a ring I plan to give to my future wife."

"Just a minute. . . . I'm confused. What are you doing here?"

The man gave Ramírez a curious look, stepped forward onto a Superlight portfolio and said, "The same as you, if you don't mind my saying so."

"Whaddaya mean?"

"I suggest you look in *that* direction. Those are the most recent ones. The workers toss the new ones down every thirty days . . . maybe you can find yours there . . . with any luck."

Ramírez turned to look at where the man was pointing. He looked all around. He got so terrified, livid with fear. *What is this place?* He couldn't breathe, his legs weakened.

"What's it like?"

"What?" Ramírez said, trying to keep from fainting.

"Your bag, of course."

"Black, with blue squares, a scotch plaid," he blurted out.

Mark looked at him and smiled, then extended his hand. Ramírez thought that Mark looked like himself.

"Welcome to Lost & Found, my friend."

" . . . "

"I hope you find what you're looking for."

Ramírez was so bewildered, he couldn't say a word. He just watched as Mark hopped from one suitcase to another like someone hopping on rocks to cross a stream. Ramírez fell to his knees, bit his tongue fiercely and closed his eyes in hopes that it all would disappear.

Instead, the image came to him of a bus taking a curve and crashing over a Mercedes and plunging into ravine, twisting and bouncing off trees and boulders, consumed by flames and smoke. Ramírez sees himself watching as his two daughters are thrown out the windows and his wife is dashed against the windshield, bleeding profusely, dying, while he desperately grabs for her hand, telling her he loves her, even though he had packed his suitcase to leave her. . . . But he can do nothing, cannot move, while his bag falls into a bottomless pit, into the darkness, the antimatter where all lost things accumulate: photos, memories, letters, ideas generated by our own emotions . . . so many things, even those that have remained unnamed.

The Day Before the Day Before

In memory of my uncle Gustavo

1

Grace always hated her job. Also the planes, the little world of the flight attendants and the lack of sleep. At times she dreamed that the machine she was flying in got crushed like a fly by the hand of a cruel God, who flung it against the clouds, but just before the crashing and the blood flowing from the skies, she'd wake up dripping in sweat.

In total air miles she had enough to circumnavigate the globe twice . . . literally. She looked at her eyes in the mirror. How many captains had she slept with? With how many stewards and first-class passengers? She adjusted the metal insignia of her airline, straightened her blouse and skirt, tied the red scarf around her neck and smiled at herself the way she would smile at the passengers boarding in two hours. She finished packing. She realized the job had lost its glamor, so had sleeping with strangers. As far as she was concerned, all captains and stewards were premature ejaculators, suffering from the effects of high altitude, the irregular hours and all that. She kept score, some twenty men all told, twenty, that wasn't too many. Some of her co-workers had exceeded a hundred, easily; some even bragged about many more. She remembered almost each one-night stand. In most cases, she agreed to sleep with them out of sheer loneliness. She didn't regret any of it. She had decided: *One day the plane goes down, and goodbye forever.* . . . She knew it, it was better in that profession to know it. She'd never forget some of those indiscretions. One in particular stood out: she had spent a wonderful, luxurious weekend with a Lebanese businessman in London, regaled by him with gifts and treated like a princess. She also remembered another time with an undercover agent who fancied himself an art collector: three days in Rome playing at being spies and enjoying great sex in a castle. There were other memorable encounters, but the one that drove her insane, for sure, was supposedly a writer she ran into on two different flights, in two different countries. He was fun, with an incredibly erotic imagination. First on a flight from Dallas, then on one from Los Angeles. These led to two unforgettable weekends . . . no one had ever touched her body like that.

2

For "Los Alacranes" (the Scorpions), last evening had been a grand slam: a full auditorium, their contract extended for gigs in the major Mexican cities of Guadalajara and San Luis Potosí in the Fall. Now, they were on the road to San Antonio and Austin—not bad for a rock band that had seen better days: two records in the top ten and handfuls of money. Women, wild nights and drugs.

The high spot came at the end of the concert when they played "Bienvenidos al Cielo" (Welcome to Heaven), when the guitar riffs sparred with the delirious drumming lighted by flashing white lights and strobes. Champagne, teenybopper female fans, front-page coverage in the newspapers of the capital, an interview on a morning TV show, invites to private parties, suitcases full of little presents.

To their surprise, the Scorpions got out of the limousine at the airport terminal with no fans to greet them, just the porters and valet parkers. They looked wilted: two of them had diarrhea, one was constipated and the lead singer had brain fog. They just weren't the same guys who used to be able to party for days on end. While the porters were unloading their luggage from the limo, they were greeted by their aging agent, hobbling up to them with a cane. Together, they all headed for Departures and passed through Security without incident. On the way to the gate they stopped in front of a store window and saw their true reflection: the grandpa of rock agents and four rancid old-timers, whose songs were only aired on oldie radio stations.

3

Pedro Manuela Madrid Ocaña woke up at his usual hour of 11 am, stretched the length of his tall body and yawned like a lion. Last night he had consumed a bottle of whiskey and snorted at least a gram of coke. He pressed a button on the remote control for the drapes to open and let in the dim light of what would be a rainy day. Lying beside him in bed, snoring, was an old lover who had been an admirer of his father, the ex-president of Mexico. Pedro got to his feet and walked across his room on the ninth floor of El Nacional hotel, where he was still welcomed. He looked out the window and saw the traffic moving slowly on the Avenida de la Reforma. He scratched his balls. He could barely make out the mountains in the distance, appearing like some phantom in a Rulfo story . . . a phantom like himself, he sighed. Twenty, twenty-five years ago, when his father had led the country, Pedro had been like a king of a "Mexico on its way to being modern," according to the historians. His nickname as a child was "Little Tiger," and it suited him well in his scandalous glory days, when he rode a powerful Harley Davidson down the Reforma, blockaded just for him and his security detail of body guards and police escort. He smiled. Yes, those were the best of times. He could still hear the fresh laughter of a radiant María Angélica, holding onto him from behind as he raced at 180 kilometers per hour . . . the picture of happiness. He closed his eyes to retain the memory. He had always wanted to remain in that time of his life . . . young, the king of the country, of the city that was all his, accompanied by the angel-faced María Angélica, who still appeared in his dreams. He sighed again. His vacation was ending and he had to return to his real life in Dallas, where he managed a new and used car lot. He was no kind of king in Dallas for sure, not even in Mexico, for sure, although he still had a lot of friends in politics and business. Not all upstanding citizens either. But that's the way things worked in Mexico, and everyone accepted it, except, of course, for the nosey journalists and the political opposition, who likewise took advantage of their parents and relatives in positions of power. As the saying goes: "Birds of a feather flock together."

4

Cristal García applied the deep red lipstick to the fleshy lips that helped make her famous as the female lead in the "Cuna de Estraños" (Nest of Strangers) soap opera, which had stayed on the air for over five years. The plot was conventional: Cristal played the poor, ingenuous, provincial orphan who found herself working in the mansion of a wealthy businessman who, by the end of the drama, discovered she was his daughter. By the fourth season she had become rich and dedicated to serving the poor, visiting small towns, building churches and maternity clinics, like a female messiah. During one of those trips, she ran into a prideful Jeremiah, an honest but impoverished man who refused her generosity as an affront to his dignity as a man. After various encounters, as would be expected, she ended up falling in love with him. "Money can buy anything, except the dignity of a Mexican" was the tear-jerker phrase that cemented the fame of Cristal García as one of the best actresses of the period. As far as she was concerned, that period of time was all too brief. And so was her fame, fortune and economic independence . . . all too brief, she lamented.

She was still pretty, even at 43, and after two surgeries and exhausting her talents. Today, no one recognized her in public and very few remembered her, with the exception perhaps of the fans of old soaps and TV series. So what, she still worked. She put on her shoes, looked at herself in the mirror, pulled in her belly, pushed up her breasts, turned to the side and looked at herself. Time had passed. She detested time, and getting old, and was just not prepared for it. She threw her light blue jacket on the bed, which she had chosen to deflect from her backside, which despite her not having had children and despite dieting had grown rather large. "Grandma's ass, goddammit!" She slapped her butt and took off.

5

Los Alacranes were on tour in South America, where they were still famous; everything arrives late in the Third World. Their music was still popular on the radio, which allowed them to continue on stage as the four rebels who had at one time filled Madison Square Garden and the Apollo. "But time is a damned guitar solo and, if you get carried away, it will consume you," Jimi Hendrix had said, bewitched by his guitar. You could say the same of Los Alacranes; the problem was that they stayed alive. They were still around to shout their old themes in dusty, provincial arenas where their magic was illumined by just twelve spotlights and a stage so narrow they'd break their necks if they tried their jumps. Of course they were tired of those gigs, the air travel in tourist class and sleeping in two-star hotels. Their middle-age bodies were covered in faded tattoos, their bellies were sagged and their prescription medicines were hidden in their suitcases away from the prying eyes of agents, club owners and the press. You could also say that their friendship had gotten stale, their relationship purely and simply a business. They hardly spoke to each other, and when they did, it was always recalling past glories: when times were different.

The telephone rang.

"What's up, motherfucker?" Tony, the lead singer, answered. "Yes, heh-heh, yes, baby. Of course. We open up, motherfucker. . . . Smashing Pumpkins. Six hundred thousand people . . . yes, man. Mexico . . . come on, what do you fucking expect, motherfucker, we are classics here. . . ."

Tony was an ex-addict, ex-alcoholic, an ex-husband, ex-father and ex-owner of a record company that went bankrupt. Tony and Bray were close friends, when they started the band while still sophomores in high school sharing their fanaticism for Jimi Hendrix, the electric guitar god. Bray was a master of guitar riffs and provided great harmony as a singer. The rest came fast, when Joe and Scoot joined the band. They were bland musicians who didn't care if the band was named The Scorpions or Dead Fish. Joe was a natural drummer and heavy banger while Scoot was an excellent bass guitarist who had inherited his musical talent from his father, a southerner. Now, these four were no longer just bangers, screamers and garblers of lyrics. Bray yawned as he read the newspaper, Tony was still on the phone with his twenty-something son and Scoot was staring out the window, as we often do when peering back through the time tunnel. It's through that tunnel that we now see this band and its present reality. Four balding old guys with paunches, flaccid muscles and haggard, fallen facial features. Four no-longer-popular musicians dressed in costumes more appropriate for youngsters. The difference between being on stage and being there in that hotel room was the same distance that now separated them from each other. Even worse, they bored each other. They no longer composed music together, only played and reworked their old hits.

Joe could no longer stand the tours, which affected him physically, made him sick. He would remain in his mansion, with its back patio and empty swimming pool, out-of-fashion furniture in the kitchen and everything else ancient and decaying. He enjoyed playing with his three dogs. He was a widower without children, had a girlfriend, few debts and enough money in the bank. You could say he was happy.

Scoot, on the other hand, loved the tours. They made him feel important, no matter what town or city, whether fast food or a good meal, to bed alone or accompanied. He was somewhat apathetic, always had been. He had had women, success, fame, all of life's desires, except for money, that is . . . he never had enough. "I'd rather be lucky," was his favorite saying.

Bray was always bored, although he looked upon touring as a vacation. He had married and divorced three times, had two children and was well set financially, with savings and investments. He was the richest of the four, although always bored, so bored in fact that he began to worry about it.

And Tony also liked touring. It was not that he liked going from one hotel to the next, packing and unpacking, running through airport terminals and sleeping poorly. In reality, all that activity really wore him out, but he still enjoyed himself.

Being on stage transformed him, it's where he became his former self again. In his private life, he belonged to a biker club, was up to his ears in debt and was crazy about young chicks—that was his undoing: the women, not girls, but young. The best days of his life were those three days when he had a different chick each night—how he missed that life.

Roger, the manager, was also considered a band member. He was the one with his feet on solid ground and understood that they needed to take advantage of what little fame they still had before no one remembered them, not even their children, who would send them to old folks homes to die. That was the real reason for the tours he arranged, much more so than the little money he made on tour. He himself was mortified of ending up in an extended care facility. "Why is fame so fleeting?" he'd ask himself repeatedly.

"Los Alacranes" knew each other so well that they had exhausted all possibility of conversation. At tours end, all that any of them wished for was to not see each other for at least three months.

Roger came to the room and gave them their boarding passes. "Come on, guys, why those long faces? It looks like a funeral. We're Los Alacranes! Let's act like it!"

The group had broken up for almost six months because of petty differences and arguments over money; now, they were back together for the money. It was Tony who had been bankrupted and motivated them to get together again, inspired by a documentary he saw on the great bands being considered for the Rock and Roll Hall of Fame.

"It's time we get back together again, guys. Let's forget about our differences and use our heads, it's about money. . . . It's not like I'm the only one who's had problems."

It all went to hell, or almost. Worth mentioning are the record company going under, Tony's heroin addiction and his recovery, a child sex-abuse scandal involving Scoot, the bottom falling out of the recording market, their royalties cut off by the legal firm that represented them . . . and in the ultimate analysis, being out of fashion.

When Tony made his pitch to them, the fame of Los Alacranes had waned, they were in deep debt and were suffering from alcoholism, obesity and loneliness. They all blamed each other but shared in a sense of failure when they were together, especially because they had not ascended to the summit of groups like the Rolling Stones or U2. Without ever articulating it, they knew what had gone wrong: simplistic songs, boring lyrics, monotonous beats. The truth was that most of their new numbers sounded the same as their past hits. The lead singer blamed the un-rocker-like attitude of the other members.

"Goddamn, you look more like a band of grandaddies. Move your asses, break the damn guitars!"

When Tony made his pitch then they accepted it: "It'll be our salvation. . . . They're still playing our biggest hits in the Third World, and they're on this nostalgia roll for bands from the 80s. Let's ride that wave. We know what we have to do. I'm not asking us to be friends again, not at all. I'm only asking that we perform together and make like a band on stage . . . for the money."

At one intersection in the time tunnel, we see them sitting in silence, not able to escape the sad reality of being in their 60s and envisioning themselves in action in front of the footlights.

6

Grace's life had slipped by without her noticing, serving soft drinks and passing out blankets. The pay was not great, and the glamour of the profession had disappeared. What was left was passing out customs forms, headsets and little bags of peanuts, and asking passengers to adjust their seatbelts. She had to smile at idiocies, flight attendant gossip and the flirting of airport personnel. Her life consisted of eating at fast food restaurants, sipping watered down drinks in boring bars and spending the night in cold, characterless hotels. She had a cruel awakening one day. She realized her daily vocabulary had been reduced to no more than thirty words: hello, thank you, my pleasure, please, as you wish, coffee or tea. Her smile was permanently frozen, he facial features a mask. She was seriously considering retiring, moving to one of those poor countries in order to stretch her dollars, sleep in a hammock, spend the days sunbathing on some beach. She had flown high, now it was time to come down and land, place her feet on solid ground.

7

Pedro Manuel Madrid Ocaña, alias Tigrillo, was born without any talent for politics or investing; in reality, he had very little talent for anything. Born with a silver spoon in his mouth and spoiled by his father, he never had to worry about anything. Always catered to by servants, waiters, gardeners, chauffeurs and helpers, he knew how to give orders, demand, insult, raise his voice. . . . He employed ten methods his mother taught him for dealing with affronts from his inferiors. And his father, Don Pedro Manuel, often said, "My son will be a leader, only born leaders have that executive tone." Don Pedro had climbed to the presidency from way below, step by step, one position of power after another. He had talent, but also was a manipulator, ascending through deals with delinquents, criminals and corrupt officials—everyone's Mexico for the select few.

Tigrillo was the youngest of six siblings, who would inherit Don Manuel's wealth via Swiss and US banks. Only three of the siblings were still alive. Clara, the only politician among them, was a senator in the national congress. Carlos was the manager of the real estate accumulated by Don Manuel during his presidency. Pedro Manuel, Jr., alias Tigrillo, now living in Texas, had wasted his part of the inheritance on women, gambling and drugs. His present visit to Mexico City had two purposes. First and most important, he had come to tap Carlos and Clara to make up for a shortfall in his finances that had brought him to the verge of bankruptcy. The second was to meet up with María Angélica whom he still loved after all those years. This, despite the fact that her parents had sent her to study abroad to keep her out of his reach.

The previous evening at a party for senators, he had talked with a retired general, who made him a proposal that could potentially change his future and solve his money problems. His brother and sister had denied him a loan. Clara didn't even receive him, after he had waited an hour. He also visited other relatives, some friends of his and friends of his father, some of whom did not even remember him. Two of them even confused him with his brother Carlos, the millionaire and wolf of a businessmen who had protected the family reputation and negotiated with the powerful. Tigrillo was the failure of the family, he had never gotten past being a "junior," a dumb junior who didn't even know how to manage the wealth plundered by his father for the family, at least his part of that wealth.

Tigrillo flagged down a cab and a bellboy helped him with his luggage. He had an appointment with the customs official he had worked with previously, although what he would propose this time was rather delicate, having been recommended by the general. They were to meet at a safehouse close to the airport. In the cab rive over, an old song by María Angélica played on the radio, with the cabby humming the catchy tune. Tigrillo remembered her performing on stage under a blue spotlight that made her look like someone from another world. María Angélica was the love of his life.

8

Cristal was the lover of an aging television producer who treated her like a princess, although he did force her to do things in bed that were distasteful and challenged her Christian morals. That decaying body of his, so necessary for her survival, was repulsive to her. She was worried that her only subsistence could actually disappear at any time and leave her helpless. She lost sleep over it and could not think of anything else. However, there seemed to be a possible solution, but she needed to hurry, before his children and two ex-wives beat her to it.

She hesitated to expose herself; she had sacrificed so much during the last six years. She owned her small apartment, the used BMW he had given her and a little bit of cash in the bank, hardly enough to last for the rest of her life. Her last paying contract had been for a toothpaste commercial, three years ago. She regretted not having taken advantage of her fifteen minutes of fame when she was on top, when she rejected appearing nude in that movie by that crazy Chilean director that was now considered a cult film. Why couldn't the clock be rewound? Why was it impossible to undo the decisions of the past? Her neighbor and partner in crime, Isabel, had come up with a pro-posal that at first seemed off the wall, the product of too much to drink. Now, she was reconsidering, it could work out.

Kidnap the old guy, make him sign some papers and then empty the safe at his house in Houston, where he had two rooms full of compromising documents and money. Of course, she couldn't pull it off by herself, she needed accomplices. Isabel searched among their friends and acquaintances for support, and now she was bringing along a phone number. Cristal drove from her walled community onto the loop circling the city. The radio was playing "Los Alacranes," and she raised the volume and began swaying to the rhythm of "El amor es una piedra que cae al río" (Love Is a Stone that Falls into the River).

She met up with Isabel and a friend of a friend, who appeared after the two of them had started talking. Isabel was gorgeous as usual, although obviously nervous.

"The stuff one has to do for a friend!" she blurted out.

Of course she was doing it out of friendship, but this time she also had her personal reasons. This would be a dry run. She was being practical, because one of her uncles, a millionaire, was close to death, and she wanted to shorten the wait time. "Practice makes perfect."

Cristal had no idea what she meant.

The "friend," an ex-cop with indigenous features, claimed to also have served on the presidential security team as an intelligence expert, trained in the School of the Americas as a hired assassin.

9

The first time that Grace had wished the plane plunge into the ocean was after she had slept with a handsome, blue-eyed captain who had treated her worse than a prostitute.

"I don't like that," she had said.

"Don't put on airs, girl, just do what I say. Who do you think you are?! What did you think, I'd ask your hand in marriage?"

Grace remembered it as if it were yesterday. She could write a book about her experiences with men. If it wasn't their giving her wilted flowers, it was expensive wine that gave her diarrhea. The first conquest on her list was an amiable Colombian who smelled of sardines and burnt cocaine; the fat man gave her a gold watch he bought on SkyMall and afterward had a limo deliver her to her next shift. Remembering smells, there was that Caribbean guy with the stench of salt, squid, eggs and beans, and rancid sweat and salty seas after the act. Men who sweet-talked you to the skies, bad jokes, blubbering, screams and finally indifference . . . or just doors closing qui etly after these machos had passed through her life, like the flights from one city to the next, cities where their wives, children and pets awaited their return. . . . But she didn't even have that: a dog wagging its tail for her any place on the planet. Her place, temporarily, was Atlanta, a city as bland as the aisles on the planes she had flown a million, two million round trips during her fifteen years as an attendant, server, escort. . . .

It had all started as a joke with that stuck-up motherfucker of a blue-eyed captain. She had confessed to him her fantasy of doing it on a plane. He said he'd take care of it. They planned it for after the plane had emptied of passengers. It was genuinely memorable, except for that jerk. Their clothes were scattered from first class to seat 35C, where they climaxed. They had swilled all the cheap wine possible, and what started out as a romantic encounter ended badly. Mr. Captain turned out to be a sadist.

10

Tony, Bray, Joe, Scoot and Roger of "Los Alacranes" took their seats in first class. A dim light created shadows in the aisle, and for a moment Tony got goose bumps at the sight of passengers with no faces. Even the flight attendant seemed to have blurred features. He realized the nightmarish vision was from lack of sleep, bad Mexican coke and just bad behavior.

Bray, an acute, intuitive observer, surmised that the passengers were groggy after having connected from a previous flight. Suddenly his whole life seemed to pass before his eyes in fast forward.

"It's fascinating. When destiny gives you all you could desire and you become a king, everyone treats you as fortunate, as if destiny has you totally covered. Under her watchful eyes, all obstacles and difficult situations are eliminated," Bray announced.

Scoot agreed with his drummer. That long trip they'd been on was nothing less than complete luck, a winning lottery ticket . . . being in the right place at the right time.

Joe sat down next to him, hoping to sleep through the flight, and popped some pills.

A flight attendant asked for seat belts to be fastened.

11

Cristal placed her carry-on bag in the compartment above and turned to look at the people occupying the next seats. She could not see their faces clearly, perhaps because of the dim lighting or because they had their faces covered. She sat down and took a deep breath. She hated flying. She felt as if her stomach were hollow, but knew it was her insecurity because of the little respect she received, at least that's what her therapist had said, that and she was always in a state of worry and dependence. That's why she had not had success. And it was too late to make real changes, perhaps because she had waited too long to decide, to act. Something in her had to change, though, and it was not easy to arrive at the realization. She was taking a flight to do a little job, but also to see a professional who could get rid of her lover; she was carrying a document to give him. She had sworn to carry out the mission without emotion. She might not love him but did feel respect and affection for him. She had to do it in order to continue to live her life as it was. What could she do without all that her lover gave her? Goodbye to luxury, to beautiful clothes and even the organic food in the refrigerator. She was fearful, of course, but that was natural and already discussed with the professional. Now, there was nothing left but to act, before her lover's children and his exes left her penniless on the street. She herself was the last link in the chain, therefore the most likely to be cut. She had never pictured herself in such a situation, but there she was, and the shoe fit . . . employing a hired killer.

"Never say never," Isabel had told her while sipping a daiquiri.

12

Grace was fed up with Atlanta, the city with the largest airport in the United States and her home base. She was fed up with her empty apartment, with its blank walls and bland furniture. She was fed up with what waited for her: an early retirement, express relationships and the unstable plans of life in the air.

Right on time that morning, like everything in her life, the airport van was there to pick her up, along with her co-workers for Flight 702 to Texas. On the way to the airport, they joked and laughed. A couple freshened their make-up, lips, nails, and straightened their insignias. Sitting next to her was Lupita, who was filled with enthusiasm because this was her third flight. Another novice, also Mexican, sat in the front seat sobbing uncontrollably, with an attack of nerves because she had a bad feeling.

In all her years, Grace had only felt fear twice. Once was during a forced landing on a football field on that infamous September 11 when two passengers had gone crazy attacking all the others. The second time was during a fierce storm, when all the passengers could be heard praying as if they were in church, holding hands and begging for life in a chorus. The plane had been bouncing about among the thunder and dark clouds enveloping the aircraft like a deadly glove.

13

Like the other characters in our story, Pedro Manuel, Jr., alias Tigrillo, also was on board Continental Flight 702 to Dallas. He took his seat in first class next to a couple of smelly long-haired old men. On the way, he had snorted four fat lines of coke given to him by the friend who dropped him off at the airport. He boarded quite high. There was a mess awaiting him in Dallas, innumerable problems that could not be addressed without funds, funds he did not have. He was fucked, it was that simple. Not only was he at risk of losing his place, but also the car dealership, which was his only income source. He had lost the houses he rented out, his investments, his businesses, his friends, his family. If things went well, he'd have a handful of documents on his desk awaiting his signature and sitting across from him one of those rabid lawyers who devour even the last bone in your body. If they went badly, there would be an enforcer holding a gun to his temple. He had just three days to pay off his debt. All his capital had been invested in the car dealership, which sold good cars to good clients: movie stars, heirs, nouveau riche and tough guys who paid in cash. He still had not figured out how he ended up doing business with those guys.

The buzz from the coke was letting him see his situation in a new light. He was clearly at the edge of the abyss. He was done for, not even a chance of returning to Mexico, where no one would come to his aid, much less receive him in their home. He had lied so often, made so many bad decisions, acted erratically, had been unstable . . . he was an idiot.

He'd order some rum from the flight attendant, what the hell.

Grace stopped at his seat to take his order.

Cristal was refreshing her makeup and deciding on the voice she'd use with the good witch.

Tony felt like some rum, although he knew seltzer water would be better for his ulcer.

Beside him, Bray was already snoring, like the rest of the rock band.

The plane took off and was soon in the air, never to touch terra firma again.

Tonatzin

1

As the train pulled up to the buffer stop, the lieutenant in charge of the operation looked out between the slats of the cattle car and heard hundreds of muffled voices sighing and praying. Cristóbal Cortés ordered the latch opened on the last car. A dead silence and the stench of humanity spread as the doors were swung open. In the shadows of the cattle car there were eyes barely visible. Lieutenant Cortés could make out some shapes moving through flashlight beams. A putrid smell wafted out that was a mix of sweat, vomit, blood and rotten bananas. A baby's screeches suddenly reverberated, and the soldiers pointed their weapons into the darkness. One of them jumped up and into the car. He stood up, confident that he was backed up by a number of his companions pointing rifles. He turned on his flashlight and began to make his way through the arms and legs crowded together in the shadows. From the rear could be heard the furious cursing in a Mayan dialect of a man's ire hardly restrained. He tried to place the voice emerging from that suffering mass that could barely raise their heads and open their eyes. He stopped in front of a man with his head ducked into his chest, unable to see the man's face. The immobile figure was tiredly leaning his frame against some empty boxes with English lettering.

"What did you say?" the soldier asked.

"Exactly what you heard," he answered without looking up.

The military man leaned over, grabbed the man by his hair and pulled him to his feet. He pulled him over to the door and asked, "Did you understand what I said?"

"You traitor," Tonatzin said to the soldier.

Two of the soldiers chambered bullets in their rifles, followed by the gasps of the people inside. The sounds echoed within the car walls and then dissipated.

"That's the way I like it, nice and quiet. But we're gonna take this foul-mouthed Indian with us . . . and thank your lucky stars we're not taking you all."

The car door was slammed shut.

2

The general in charge of the Matamoros region resented what the cartel was paying and decided to take a lion's share instead. He'd pull out one migrant per boxcar so they'd know who the boss was.

The officer in charge of doing his bidding, Lieutenant Cristóbal Cortés, would receive a measly percentage for executing the migrant pulled from each one of the cars. A single shot was heard ten times, one for each car. The same operation as if it was being rehearsed. Cortés ordered three soldiers to dig a mass grave to the sound of screams and cries.

"If you stupid broads don't shut up, I'll shoot you all right now, and that'll be the end of it!" Cortés yelled.

And then there was a deadly silence.

3

Tonatzin was traveling in the last car of the train. From the very first shot and the cries that followed he realized it was an execution. He knew that at least one of the migrants heading for the USA was going to die, and maybe he'd be the one. Tonatzin, who had night vision, witnessed on each man's face the rage of stifled terror.

It was now his car's turn, and the door slid open. A flashlight beam cut through the darkness inside. Death let loose looked at each face with disdain. The migrant men swallowed hard, and the women shrunk back. The fear of being chosen by the executioner and God's grace blurred the features of each shrinking face. With one exception: the stone face of Tonatzin, who challenged the soldier in the Mam language of his ancestors from Guatemala.

The sergeant made his way through the sprawled bodies, stopped in front of Tonatzin and lifted him up. From the tightly packed mass of migrants Tonatzin arose and took a step forward, whereupon the soldier grabbed him by the neck and pushed him to the open door.

Lieutenant Cortés yelled for them to get down. The soldiers there were ready and willing to shoot.

Tonatzin leaped to the ground and, after not having moved his legs for a few days, he fell hard on the gravel by the tracks.

The soldiers thought his being on all fours was a sign of fear, and one of them hit him with his rifle butt to get him to stand up. Tonatzin's natural reaction was to get up and punch, bite and curse the cowardly bunch who were gripping their weapons tightly. In two quick movements, he was up from the ground.

4

Lieutenant Cortés stepped up to a faceless man . . . or at least that was the impression he had of the short, leathery Indian with the big mouth. He ordered one of his men to train a flashlight on Tonatzin's face. What he saw was an arrogant smile on a dark face that dared look him straight in the eyes. He thought for an instant he remembered that look, that face, but his memory failed. He was almost positive he had seen those bloodshot eyes that were piercing, challenging, undressing him.

In Lieutenant Cortés' eyes Tonatzin saw lust, vice and sadism. Of course, he remembered the lieutenant who had led the massacre of his Mayan community at Comalcalco. One of his soldiers had given Tonatzin a nickname relating to his ethnicity, a bad joke that only they understood and laughed at. To his ears, their laughter sounded infantile, almost primitive.

Tonatzin's insolent voice echoed in the dark. "What would you say, Lieutenant, if I said you're about to die?" He looked around at the rest of the squad. "Did you know that you're all about to die?" he said to the soldiers who were not accustomed to their victims speaking directly to them with such aggression.

Only a couple of them, however, understood what their captive had said to them in Mam and took a step back. The Indian seemed to be very sure of what he was saying.

"What is this damn Indian saying?"

"Did you know, you bunch of assassins . . . ," Tonatzin said slowly as if enjoying each syllable, this time in clear Spanish, "that you are going to die tonight?"

One of the soldiers lifted his eyes to the heavens.

"Yes, tonight you are going to meet your maker," Tonatzin said—this time in English.

"Shut the fuck up, asshole!" a corporal barked as he stepped up and smashed his rifle butt into Tonatzin's face.

Tonatzin sank to his feet, bleeding.

"Get up, asshole!" the corporal said as two other soldiers pushed the muzzles of their AR-15s into his ribs.

"Fuckin' Indian can't see who's holding the rifles. . . . I bet you've got it wrong who's gonna die," Lieutenant Cortés warned at the front of the squad.

He was still unable to see Tonatzin's face. He seemed to recognize his body type and powerful, vibrant voice. *Where have I seen this Indian bastard?*

"Get up, didn't you hear?!" the corporal yelled as he pulled Tonatzin up by his shirt collar and pointed a pistol to his head.

Tonatzin recovered, swallowed saliva mixed with blood and felt totally helpless. He recalled his people being massacred, the women raped, their communities wiped off the map.

"Yes, I'm sure I'm about to die, it does not matter," he said, wiping the blood streaming from the corner of his mouth.

Cortés felt like emptying his pistol's clip into his head just to see who laughed last.

He stepped closer to the Indian, whose bloodshot, arrogant eyes continued to challenge him and said, "Start running . . . in any direction." He looked at him, then at his squad and then into the dark surroundings.

"Run? Where? If you're going to kill me, do it here. Why should I run?"

"Run, asshole, that's an order!"

"You can give orders to your men. Me, I don't need to run to find death," Tonatzin countered, crossing his arms over his chest and looking around at the squad.

"Run, don't run, you're still a runner to us, you coward! Anyway, who knows, maybe you'll escape, Indian asshole!"

"Yeah, and maybe our bullets will miss you," the corporal sarcastically seconded his superior.

"Maybe you can duck and avoid the bullets in the dark," the sergeant added as he chambered a bullet.

"Yeah, maybe you'll get out of this alive," Lieutenant Cortés said. "Now, run, fucker!!"

"Where?"

"Wherever. . . . It'll be better, believe me, there's always a chance you'll get lucky."

Cortés smiled and looked at his men, then at the little man whose eyes had turned completely white as if he were on the verge of a seizure. "I'll count to three."

With that, Tonatzin turned into a shadow with an electric current seeming to course through his body, and he took off running into the darkness of the night as if he had been shot out a cannon. As he ran in circles around the soldiers, they fired blindly, even hitting each other. After successfully avoiding every single bullet, Tonatzin stopped and approached Cortés, who was lying wounded on the ground. It was hard for Cortés to understand what had happened. The shadow smiled at him as it disappeared into the night in a circular pattern.

Cat Life

1

One of those unexpected events, amazing in reality, happened to Mrs. Robbins in Philadelphia. Luis Carmona was a boarder in Robbins' house, and it just so happened that she was crazy about cats. She kept at least fifteen kitties who she named after the Apostles—she had a couple of Pauls and Ezequiels—although Carmona never understood how she went about baptizing them. She went to the extreme of believing the cats to be from another world, that is reincarnations of deceased people or ghostly projections. Carmona blithely attributed it to the strange ideas of old people.

Carmona rented one of four rooms in the basement that the aged woman rented out, but he never met the other boarders, although at times he did hear them coming and going. It was true that he got the room for a really good price, and the location was also pretty good; the area was quiet on weekends. The room was a little humid, with windows reaching the ceiling and mildew in the bathroom, but it had a large closet and a rear door that led to a garden. And when he wanted to avoid Mrs. Robbins or just didn't feel like socializing with animals, he'd go out back. He had his landlord's permission to occasionally take a chair out to the garden and enjoy the plants; as a child he had worked with his family as a migrant farm worker in Texas and he still appreciated the fragrance of things growing. Carmona at the time was working construction and sending money to his mother back in Oklahoma. He had to struggle to find work, like his parents and uncles, and was happy to be working for this Texas firm that built office buildings in various cities. Pay was decent, the work not too hard, he was gaining experience and supervised a few workers. He believed in hard work, not in magic or the esoteric. That's why what happened to him was really frightening.

Carmona was the type of person who could adapt to circumstances, in this case the cats and their many distinct personalities. He adopted a yellow one he perceived to be the least loved by the landlord. The cat was good at defending himself from the other cats, so Carmona named him "Leoncito," that is Little Lion. He began buying the cat food and letting the cat share his bed at night.

The night of the "event," which is how he refers to it, the cats were his witnesses. He doesn't remember what he was thinking at the time, but suddenly his hands fell asleep and the numbness traveled to his extremities and then his entire torso. When he had lost almost all control of his senses, he panicked. *Am I having a stroke? I'm too young for that. What else could it be? Am I poisoned? Maybe because of all those years as youngster breathing in fertilizer. Or maybe the stench of cat urine?* He asked himself many things while staring at the cats.

"Calm down," he said to himself out loud. He needed to take it easy and stop panicking, which was the worst thing he could do.

He closed his eyes, tried to control his fear. He tried so hard that he heard something "crack" in his head. But according to his ears the silence was complete. *Maybe I'm dead*

... *or dying.* He opened his eyes again, and he was levitating, he was in the air floating above everything as if he had been freed from gravity. He was floating horizontally a few feet over the bed and able to see out the window to the street. He saw a woman walking as she spoke on her cell phone, and there was the neighbor from two houses over who was walking her dog, a black German shepherd that smelled cats in the vicinity and was marking his territory by urinating everywhere. The dog came to the window and saw him floating, stretched out horizontally in the air. The dog didn't think much of it, lifted a leg, pissed on the window and then trotted after his owner. A car passed in slow motion. The mailman with his bag on his shoulder crossed the street and disappeared in the doorway of the neighbors across the street. Two men on bikes also crossed his field of vision.

The cats observed him with curiosity. Only a couple of them understood that he was floating; the others licked their whiskers, sucked on their paws or tails, were bored by the scene as if nothing strange had happened or were lounging belly up.

At first, he thought he was hallucinating and was terrified. "Calm down," he told himself again. His grandmother had taught him that you could control fear, channel it, as long as you didn't panic. Carmona arrived at the conclusion that he was indeed floating in the air in his room, despite all logic. He looked around. Yep, to his surprise, he was in the air, freed from gravity like an astronaut. Once he controlled his fear, he pushed on a wall and floated toward the bathroom, and then started floating all around the room. He felt light as a feather, and he could see everything from above, peering from the ceiling down to the floor. Weightless, he spent a few minutes pushing himself from one wall to another. Free of the gravitational pull, he also lost the rigidity of his body. He tumbled around in the air, enjoying himself until he tired.

He doesn't remember how things got back to normal. The cats left, and he finally had to get into bed. He was exhausted, as if he had run a few kilometers. These unfastenings, as he started calling them, continued to reoccur.

2

During the last night at his apartment, around 3 am. Carmona sensed he was being watched and carefully opened his eyes in the dark. He was still floating, although not very high, just a few inches. He realized the fifteen cats were staring at him—thirty eyes shining in the dark. It was very strange. At first he shrank in fear at all those neon eyes watching him intently, but then realized that they belonged to the kitties. They stared without blinking, as if they knew he was about to leave the house or something. Was it that his time had run out in that house, where these ghostly creatures would stay to take charge and live freely?

He grabbed the headboard of his bed and slowly pulled himself down to sit on the bed. They continued to watch him, and he them—it was some type of communication unfamiliar to him, perhaps some sort of affection among animals.

Carmona was fascinated.

Some of the cats were seated on the bed, the chest of drawers, his desk and on the backrest of his chair, all seated around the room in various positions. He was surrounded. A couple of the most daring ones came up to Carmona and began to purr softly as he petted their backs in a show of friendship.

Carmona understood that they had come to say goodbye and wish him good luck. He wasn't sure if they repeated the gesture every time one of Mrs. Robbins guests were departing or if they considered him special. Some of the cats kept their distance but from their perches contributed to the collective purring, which made the contents of the room vibrate. The purring was rhythmic and in unison.

Today, from the distance of another city and a different context, Carmona still envisions the scene of the landlord's cats and their eyes shining in that old house's bedroom. All around him those eyes shining on the last night he spent there.

That the cats were in his room was not only a farewell but also a presage. Little Lion, the cat he had adopted for its friendliness, looked into Carmona's eyes from a few inches away, as if looking inside for his soul. At one point when he was able to communicate with them, no matter where they were perched in the room, they let him know their desire to share a dream with him. In the dream, Carmona was a cat, and that's when he woke up.

In the dream, Carmona ambles through a brilliant blue forest. He's a nocturnal animal. From the ground he is able to leap up and climb a tree by digging his claws into the trunk. He reaches the tallest branch of the tree and, embraced by the leaves, can see all around. In the distance he can see a town on the other side of the great wall and another forest. He makes his way along the branch, tenses and then leaps to the next tree, and then to the next, and the next. He briefly looks back to see the great distance he's traveled. He's proud of his progress, which encourages him to continue jumping from tree to tree. He's aware of the danger, although he is enjoying the adrenalin and testosterone rush. He continues jumping, flying through the air, defying gravity. He has another mission in mind, and as he crosses through the darkness he can see that he has the advantage of surprise, and after a great leap through space lands on all fours.

The Apparently Abandoned
God-Forsaken City

for Juan Rulfo

1

According to the clairvoyant's crystal ball, we were supposed to die on our attempt to cross the wall. We were close to it, and death was everywhere enticing us, perched on a cactus, mumbling obscenities in our ears, manifesting in the frigid breeze.

Suddenly I found myself surrounded by complete darkness and murmuring. I was on my haunches, still dripping water from the Río Grande after crossing the border. There was an electrified fence a few meters high and the wall extended far off to my left and right. I paused, looked around and was able to stick my head through a hole in the steel wall. In horror, I saw that dead bodies were strewn everywhere. Someone pushed me from behind to hurry up. I had to go on through, that was my destiny, and my fleeing companions were at my heels.

We started running, effortlessly jumping over bodies and avoiding graves awaiting us, zigzagging to evade the infrared cameras and rifle scopes of our hunters. We had been advised to not look back, that whoever did would perish. We ran a long stretch, cracking the dried, sun-bleached bones beneath our feet. We crossed the desert, aided by the clouds covering the moon. Quietly. Each one on his own in a cold sweat, all five sense at peak alert, swallowing clouds of dust, heading off toward an uncertain destiny . . . cutting through shadows. Looking for work.

2

"Hey, Nacho, what's up? How you doin'?"

"Good, my brother. You?"

"Good, you know, working . . . working."

"Hmm, yeah, me too, brother. What else is new?"

"Your hands, Nacho? Where are your hands?!"

"I left them at work on the other side, bro . . . you know, to make some money."

3

Waves of immigrants: brown, black, yellow and shades in between, invading everywhere, arriving on our shores in giant truck inner tubes, small rafts, inflatable boats, aircraft . . . packed together like merchandise, like livestock on trains. . . . Immigrants of all the dark skin tones. Coming from all the continents and all the islands. Immigrants. People on the move, who knows from where or why, with children, with families, toward the First World, their eyes squinting, speaking sharply accented florid and complex languages, carrying handfuls of spices, rusty spoons, tattered clothing, knives. Hundreds, thousands, millions of people, with fortune cookies in their pockets and grains of rice stuck between their teeth. People of corn, of potatoes, they are scarecrows with souls. Many now buried, having died of hunger on their way from Latin America, Africa, Asia. An invasion. Taking the

First World by assault, like a dark fever; poverty, plague and Nostradamus' millennial prophecy: ". . . the third world, introduced and sustained by a fork, will become rooted . . ."

4

Whenever I get scared, I grab my balls. At the most terrifying, most exciting or surprise moments, that's where you'll find my hand. It's instinctive, I guess, that my hands treat the testicles as a lifesaver or a piece of lumber floating in the ocean that a shipwrecked person grabs. How can I explain it? Does it happen to you? It's as if my hand and my gonads comfort each other. That's how I understand it. The truth is that there's no one in this selfish and bizarre world of the twenty-first century who will save you, if not for yourself . . . sadly, you learn that early on.

Holding onto myself, I face the world and proceed.

5

There's an old saying that once you've gotten what you wished, you lose interest in it and soon forget it. What's worse, you start to wish for something else. Something like that happens with cities. After you've spent a few months or even years in a city, and you know how to get around to fill your daily needs, the city becomes a background for more important things: daily life, work life, real life, making money. That is, what's new becomes old hat and lasts about as long as a match flame. From getting to know the city we become indifferent to it, become bored, tired, embarrassed. Repetition trivializes, and what's new gets old. You are no longer a tourist in the new land, captivated by what's different and nervous about the unknown. He who is fascinated with the landscape out the bus's window, sleeps on the return trip.

Finally and after trying repeatedly, I have shed a part of me.

Whoever says you can't live in two places at the same time is dead wrong. I am looking at you with a smiley face, while with my other face I'm looking at the thousands of photos I carry in my pockets—and you have no idea about it—always thinking about moving to a new place, a new city.

6

I'm stopped at a traffic light, here in New York. To be specific, the taxicab I drive is stopped, just like the other taxis and cars driven by people like me, the majority of whom are immigrants, outsiders, and therefore people in transit, as usual. They are common everyday people trying to make a living in the concrete jungle of skyscrapers, from which we are observed, scanned, photographed and judged. We're observed by cameras installed on the streets and drones that patrol the city. We're heard by microphones installed on our cell phones and studied by a select group of special people who, way above ground level, enjoy their offices of expensive furniture and deep piled carpets while they look upon us as if we're mice scurrying to our warrens.

New York reaches to the sky, and New York digs deep below skyscrapers and the subway. The streets are full of us: men dirty from manual labor and with wallets bereft. The others who look down upon us delight in seeing us as ants struggling over a piece of bread. Those above, the ones who decide on the future of the world, divide up among themselves the natural resources and decide on their use. We down here can't see the world from our caves, our humid and dark basement apartments, our dilapidated attic rental rooms filled with roaches, mice and other pests, eating garbage and processed foods rich in fat, flour and cholesterol. What can I say: that's genetically modified food for you, food from laboratories, from experiments, food for the poor, the thousands of little tiny creatures moving along the streets.

We make slow progress driving up and down the congested avenues, taking passengers from one side of the island to the other. Another traffic light.

I was searching for clients, driving in what looked like an abandoned city.

7

So I'm finally here in my filthy, ridiculously tiny kitchen, wearing Chinese slippers and three-day-old dirty underwear, wrapped in a grey bathrobe, telling you my life story. Out my window, New York with one building on top of the next, wall to wall. So now, I think about the real story that my hands are typing, a story I write with my eyes wide open. I stand up, walk, pace around the room. I'm stuck, floating in this new town, where I'm an intruder looking out the corner of my window, waiting patiently for the pizza delivery guy.

I'm restraining myself from saying ugly things: "Your mother said that you didn't say a word until you were six years old . . . that when you were about to be born, some Bible salesmen knocked on the door and they were ignored." You mother died holding onto a dirty bedsheet, praying to God, while your grandmother was giving you mouth to mouth resuscitation and spanking you with her calloused hands.

As I'm adjusting my pants and putting on my jacket, it stops raining and it gets dark outside. The street vendors all disappear on Sundays. I remember my mother, my sister, my town, my childhood. . . . I return through the time tunnel as if the rain has awakened me from a dream. I'm soaked. Maybe it's because of this that I utter a string of blasphemous curses as I climb down the stairs of the rent-controlled building where I live and where a developer wants to evict us. There is graffiti on the walls I can't decipher.

New York without friends, without family, without a future. In my new home, which is nothing less than the guts of Manhattan Island. . . . Although I hate to admit it, I'm a real flesh and blood Jonah in the belly of the whale that floats on the Hudson. I travel in two languages. As I get out into the street, I zip up my jacket and light a cigarette. Two steps forward, two steps backward, and the pizza delivery guy has not come.